My mind was racing. "Okay, here's the plan. We'll pull all our troops back to the porch and set up a line of defense. If he leaves, we won't bark. If he tries to enter the house, we'll hit him with everything we've got. What do you think?"

Zoom! Drover was already streaking toward the porch like a little comet, leaving me out in front of the house without reserves. I wheeled around, hit Turbo Four, and made a dash for the porch.

When I got there, Drover was huddled behind Slim's chair. "Coward! Get out from behind that chair." He didn't move, so I did what any normal American dog would have done. I pushed and shoved and joined him behind the chair.

There, in our foxhole on the front lines, we huddled together and listened to the sound of the stranger's footsteps. *He was coming toward the house!*

The Case of
the Secret Weapon

HANK
THE COWDOG®

The Case of
the Secret Weapon

John R. Erickson

Illustrations by Gerald L. Holmes

PUFFIN BOOKS
An Imprint of Penguin Group (USA) Inc.

PUFFIN BOOKS
Published by the Penguin Group
Penguin Young Readers Group, 345 Hudson Street, New York, New York 10014, U.S.A.
Penguin Group (Canada), 90 Eglinton Avenue East, Suite 700, Toronto, Ontario,
Canada M4P 2Y3 (a division of Pearson Penguin Canada Inc.)
Penguin Books Ltd, 80 Strand, London WC2R 0RL, England
Penguin Ireland, 25 St Stephen's Green, Dublin 2, Ireland
(a division of Penguin Books Ltd)
Penguin Group (Australia), 250 Camberwell Road, Camberwell,
Victoria 3124, Australia (a division of Pearson Australia Group Pty Ltd)
Penguin Books India Pvt Ltd, 11 Community Centre,
Panchsheel Park, New Delhi - 110 017, India
Penguin Group (NZ), 67 Apollo Drive, Rosedale, North Shore 0632,
New Zealand (a division of Pearson New Zealand Ltd.)
Penguin Books (South Africa) (Pty) Ltd, 24 Sturdee Avenue,
Johannesburg 2196, South Africa

Registered Offices: Penguin Books Ltd, 80 Strand, London WC2R 0RL, England

Published simultaneously in the United States of America
by Viking Children's Books and Puffin Books,
divisions of Penguin Young Readers Group, 2010

1   3   5   7   9   10   8   6   4   2

CIP DATA IS AVAILABLE UPON REQUEST

Puffin Books ISBN 978-0-14-241511-5

Hank the Cowdog® is a registered trademark of John R. Erickson.
Printed in the United States of America

To George and Karen

CONTENTS

CHAPTER ONE

A Bed Has One Foot but No Legs

It's me again, Hank the Cowdog. The adventure began in July, as I recall. Yes, it was the Fourth of July, and Drover and I were spending a few days at Slim's bachelor shack on the banks of Wolf Creek.

Normally, we work out of our bedroom/office under the gas tanks at Ranch Headquarters, but now and then we enjoy hanging out at Slim's place. For one thing, he has no cats, so the Nuisance Factor drops to zero. That's a big plus right there. It's common knowledge that 87 percent of all the problems in this world are caused by cats. No cats, no problems.

For another thing, Slim is a bachelor cowboy, a generous soul who doesn't mind letting his dogs

1

stay inside the house. In fact, I think he enjoys having us around. He's the kind of man who talks to his dogs and sometimes he even shares his supper with us. Slim's suppers aren't always a great experience (he eats a lot of canned mackerel sandwiches), but show me a man who talks to his dogs, and I'll show you a man with refined taste and deep intelligence.

But the point is that Drover and I were spending the night at Slim's place, stretched out on the living room floor. Or let's put it this way. We *started* the night stretched out on the living room floor, but sometime in the early morning hours ...

His carpet was old and thin, don't you see, and after several hours, I woke up and couldn't go back to sleep. I tried to scratch up a soft spot, but threadbare carpet doesn't offer much in the scratching-up department.

At that point, I did what any normal, healthy American dog would have done. I crept down the long hallway to Slim's bedroom and ... well, checked out the accommodations, let us say. See, Slim slept in a bed and beds are pretty nice places to, uh, spend a long night. Heh heh.

Hovering beside the bed in the inky black ink of the darkness, I lifted my ears and took a reading on Earatory Scanners. I heard ... you know, my first thought was that someone had driven a truck into the house, but that didn't make sense. I took another reading and came up with a more reasonable answer.

Slim was snoring. Yes, he was a champion snorer, and that's what he was doing. Good. If he was snoring, he was asleep. Heh heh. This gave me the signal to begin a procedure we call Enter the Bed.

It's a pretty complicated procedure, and most of your ordinary mutts wouldn't take the time to do it. They'll just go blundering into the bed and hope for the best, but what usually happens is that the dog gets yelled at and sent out of the room.

Not me, fellers. I take the time to do it right. By George, if you can't do it right, with patience and loving care, you shouldn't do it at all.

Here's the procedure. You might want to take some notes.

Okay, you start by placing one paw on the bed. I prefer the right front paw, but the left front might work just as well. You place it on the bed, press down, and wait for a response. If you get no response, you move deeper into the program, placing the other front paw on the bed.

This is where it gets complicated. You have to transfer all the weight of your body from your back legs, which are still on the floor, to your front legs, which are in position on the bed. This step in the procedure works better if you have a set of enormous muscular shoulders, and I do.

In the Weight Transfer Sequence, you shift all your weight from back legs to front legs, lift the hind legs off the floor, and give them a soft landing on the surface of the bed. If the mission has to be scrubbed, it will usually come at this crucial point, when your full weight is balanced on the edge of the bed.

It was a very tense moment. I activated Earatory Scanners and studied the monitor that showed Slim's heartbeat, breathing patterns, and brain waves. All the signs appeared to be normal. But then . . .

This came as a shock. Just as everything appeared to be normal, Slim hiccupped in his sleep! HICK! No kidding. It came as such a surprise, I almost canceled the mission. I mean, normal people don't hiccup in their sleep, do they?

Well, Slim did and you can put that one into the record books. It almost wrecked the mission, but I managed to keep control of things. I stood my ground and didn't move a hair, and Slim went back to his normal snoring pattern.

Whew! That was a close call.

At that point, I went into Stealthy Creep and began inching my way...huh? Holy smokes, in the deep darkness at the foot of Slim's bed, I encountered some kind of creature...a carbon-based lifeform...something with hair and a doggish odor!

I froze. Every hair on the back of my neck stood straight up. Who could it be? A stray dog from town? A prowling coyote that had somehow managed to break into Slim's house and crawl into his bed? I did a quick search of our databases, looking for the names of anyone I might want to encounter on Slim's bed in the middle of the night.

My search turned up nothing. There was absolutely nobody that I wanted to meet at this particular time and place.

So what does a guy do in this situation? Run? Attack? Bark? I was in the process of weighing these options when I heard a voice in the darkness. "Oh, hi. What are you doing here?"

I melted with relief. I mean, you've seen what happens to ice cream on a blistering hot day, right? That was me. All the muscles in my highly conditioned body released their tension, and I became a puddle of a doglike substance.

Can you guess who it was? Drover. I didn't

know whether to be sad, mad, or glad. After a moment of brittle silence, I whispered, "What are you doing here, you little sneak?"

"Well . . . I couldn't sleep on that hard floor."

"What? That's ridiculous! Drover, we are the elite troops of the ranch's Security Division, and we sleep wherever we fall at the end of the day."

"Yeah, but I didn't figure Slim would mind if I borrowed part of his bed. It's a pretty nice bed."

"Of course it's a nice bed, but it's not for dogs."

"I'll be derned. What are you doing here?"

There was a moment of silence. "I was conducting a routine patrol of the promises."

"You mean the premises?"

"What?"

"You said you promised to parole the premises."

"That's correct, and in the process of doing that, I caught you trespassing on Slim's bed. Drover, I ought to throw the book at you! Do you have any idea what would happen if Slim woke up and caught us here?"

"Reckon he'd be mad?"

"Course he would. At the very least, he'd kick us out of bed. At the worst, he might throw us out of the house. Is that what you want, to become a homeless waif?"

"Well, I sure like cookies."

"What?"

"I like cookies."

"Yes, and so what? Everyone likes cookies."

"Well, you said something about vanilla wafers."

I took a slow breath of air and searched for patience. "Drover, I said 'homeless waif,' not vanilla wafer. A waif is not a cookie."

"Yeah, I think about 'em all the time. I even dream about cookies."

I stuck my nose in his face. "Stop talking about cookies. The point is that you're taking up *my* space on Slim's bed."

"Gosh, you mean ..."

"Yes. The Head of Ranch Security needs a good night's sleep."

"Well, there's plenty of room. Maybe we could share. I promise to be good."

I gave that some thought. "I suppose it might work. We'll curl up at the foot of the bed."

I heard him giggle. "Foot of the bed. That's a funny way to put it."

"What's funny?"

"Well, how can a bed have a foot if it doesn't have a leg?"

"Drover, if a bed has a foot, it must have a leg."

"Where is it?"

"I don't know. I don't care. What's your point?"

"Well, a table has four legs but no feet. A bed has one foot and no legs. Somehow that doesn't make sense."

"Look, pal, you can either make sense or sleep on the bed. Which will it be?"

"Well . . . sleep, I guess, but I still say . . ."

"Hush. Shut your little trap and go to sleep."

Whew. At last he shut his trap. I curled up at the foot of the bed and went . . . you know what? I couldn't sleep—because I couldn't stop thinking about Drover's ridiculous question: How can a bed have a foot if it doesn't have a leg to stand on?

You see what he does to me? In my deepest heart, I DIDN'T CARE, but I couldn't slink a wick all nerp and . . . swamping honk the snickle-fritzzzzzzzzz . . .

CHAPTER TWO

Morning at Slim's Shack

Okay, maybe I finally dozed off and managed to bag a few hours' sleep on Slim's bed. It was exactly the kind of peaceful sleep every loyal dog dreams about and deserves. But let the record show that I don't care why a bed has a foot but no legs.

I awoke sometime after dawn, lifted my head, and glanced around. Fresh morning light poured through the open window, and I heard the gobble of wild turkeys outside, a sure sign of a new day. Turkeys gobble and twitter in the morning when they leave their roost, don't you see, and then they go trudging off to work, pecking seeds and chasing grasshoppers.

I opened my jaws, threw a curl into my tongue, and was about to pull in a big yawn of fresh air when I noticed the head and face of a man, right beside me. I looked closer and was able to put a name with the face.

It was Slim Chance, a friend of mine. In fact, he was the guy who owned the bed.

I wasn't surprised to find him in his own bed, but you might have already picked up an interesting clue. I had gone to sleep *at his feet* but had awakened *beside his face*. In other words, sometime in the night, the bed had reversed itself, and that was pretty amazing.

You'd think that I would have noticed. I mean, Slim was a pretty big man and . . .

Wait. There was another explanation. Sleeping beside the master's face is the kind of thing a loyal dog sometimes does without thinking about it or even knowing about it. I mean, we care so deeply about our people that we just want to be close to them, and the deeper we care, the closer we want to be.

And soft pillows are kind of nice, too. Hee hee.

The problem is that . . . well, our people don't always appreciate having a sleeping dog in their faces. I had a feeling that Slim wouldn't be thrilled to find me sharing his pillow, and we sure didn't need to start a new day with him half-asleep and mad.

In other words, I needed to make a graceful exit before he woke up and caught me sleeping on his pillow.

I began creeping backward, away from the pillow, past his rib cage and bony knees, and down to the region where his feet lived. There, I tapped a paw on the sleeping Drover and whispered, "Return to base!"

He glanced around, blinked his eyes, and nodded, and together we slithered off the foot of the bed and tiptoed down the long hallway. When Slim emerged from his bedroom two hours later (it was a holiday, so he slept late), the entire Security Division was curled up asleep on the threadbare carpet.

Heh heh. Old Slim never suspected a thing, although he did mutter something about "sleeping crooked" and having a crick in his neck.

It's always interesting to watch Slim first thing in the morning. I mean, he moves like someone who is half-blind, half-dead, and walking underwater. Here he came, creeping down the hall in his boxer shorts and a T-shirt, dragging his feet across the floor while his left hand felt its way along the wall. His eyes were red-rimmed and half-shut, his hair was down in his eyes, and he had pillow tracks on one side of his face.

He finally made it to the living room, but he didn't speak to us. At this time of day, he rarely speaks. If he tries to establish any kind of communication, it takes the form of grunting sounds, but on this particular morning, he didn't even bother to grunt a greeting.

Sliding his bare feet across the floor and holding one hand out in front of him, he made his way into the kitchen and headed straight for the device that would bring him out of the vapors—a pan of water that sat on one of the burners of his propane cookstove.

A lot of people make coffee in a coffeepot or an electric perpetrator . . . perpenator . . . what's the word I'm searching for? PERCOLATOR, there we go, an electric coffee percolator. Not Slim. He has nothing but scorn for such modern devices. He boils his coffee in a pan of water.

Why? Because that's The Cowboy Way. He calls it "campfire coffee," honest coffee made over an honest fire.

With awkward, sleep-numbed fingers, he turned

on the gas, struck a match, and held it to the stove burner. The match blew out, so he struck another match and poked it under the pan.

This produced a small explosion. See, if you leave a stove burner going for ten or fifteen seconds and then add a lighted match, the propane fumes will say POOF! How do I know? I've seen him do it a hundred times, and you know what? It always makes a little explosion, and it always seems to surprise him.

Well, once he had the fire going under the pan of water, he felt his way across the cabinets above the sink until he found the same big red can of coffee he'd used the day before, in exactly the same spot on the shelf.

Most people would use a measuring spoon to transfer the ground-up coffee into the pan. Slim *dumps* it. Sometimes he gets the right amount with one dump, but sometimes it takes two or three. This time, he used one dump and two sprinkles, but the important thing is that even when he's half-asleep, he has an idea in his mind of how much coffee is just the right amount—and he doesn't need a measuring spoon to do it.

Once he had finished the Coffee Dump, he began the next phase: waiting for the water to boil. It always gets funny here, because he HATES to wait for water to boil. There he stood, blinking his soggy eyes, yawning, shuffling his feet, shaking his head, and muttering under his breath.

After a while, the water hissed and boiled, and the excitement started to build. He could smell the coffee now, and his eyes began to open up. He waited, watched, shook the pan, and at exactly the right moment, he pulled it off the stove and poured the steaming liquid into a big brown mug.

He lifted the mug to his nose, took a deep sniff, slurped down his first gulp, and growled, "Oh yeah, there it is! Let the day begin!" At that point, he spit out some coffee grounds and was ready to face the world.

Walking with bolder steps now, and without leaning against a wall, he made his way into the living room and spoke his first words to us. "Dogs, the master of the house has just arrove."

Drover and I exchanged glances. What were we supposed to do?

"Y'all could show a little more excitement."

I thumped my tail on the floor, and Drover wiggled his stub tail. If Slim expected more than that . . . well, too bad.

He scowled. "A man gets no respect these days, even from his dogs." He took another swig of coffee. "Hey, today's the Fourth of July. I've got the whole day off, and I can do whatever I want. And you know what I'm going to do?"

He seemed to be talking to me, so I went to the telegraph key of my tail and tapped out a reply. "No. What are you going to do?"

He winked. "I'm going to spend my day just like the rich and famous. I'm going to sit out on the porch in my underwear, drink coffee, and loaf. What do you think of that, pooch?"

I tapped out another reply. "That sounds pretty exciting. No doubt you'll need our help, so we'll go with you."

"Come on. I'm fixing to show you how to behave when you're wealthy and influential." He held the screen door open for us, and we all moved out on the porch.

It wasn't much of a porch because . . . well, it wasn't much of a house, but the porch had a nice view of the creek and it was big enough to hold one man, two dogs, and a couple of chairs. Slim flopped down in one of the chairs, slurped his coffee, and gazed out at the little world in front of his house.

"Dogs, life don't get any better than this—sitting on the porch in your underwear, drinking coffee, and listening to the birds. Shucks, it's a cowboy's dream." He thought about that for a moment. "You know, a guy could make a song out of that. What would y'all think if I sang you a song? Would you like that?"

I was stunned. Another of his corny songs?

We've discussed Slim's singing, right? I'm sure we have, because this had happened before. See, he comes up with these silly songs, and who or whom do you suppose has to listen to them?

Us. His dogs. I mean, we work hard, try to do our jobs and be loyal friends, but the terrible truth is that WE DON'T LIKE HIS MUSIC. There, I've said it. He's a nice man, but our lives would be complete if we didn't have to listen to his pathetic little songs.

I shot a glance at Drover and saw that he had a look of pain on his face. He whispered, "I guess we're trapped."

"I guess we're *not*. Let's see if we can slip out of here."

Drover grinned. "I never thought of that. Maybe he won't notice."

"Shhh. We'll have to be as quiet as a mouse."

"Yeah, or two mice, 'cause there's two of us."

"Good point. We'll be as quiet as two mice."

Without making a sound, we lifted our respective bodies off the porch and began oozing away from the guy who was fixing to destroy the morning silence with so-called music. If we could make it to the porch steps, we might be able to slither ourselves into the cedar shrubs and vanish without a . . .

"Hey! Come back here!"

We froze in our tracks, only inches away from the first step to Freedom. Drover rolled his eyes around to me. "Uh-oh, what do we do now?"

"We got caught, and we have to face the music. Let's get it over with and try to look professional."

Holding our heads at a professional angle, we marched back to Slim's chair and into the glare of his eyes. He was scowling, don't you see, and he grumbled, "Where did y'all think you were going? Didn't you hear what I said?"

I went to Slow Puzzled Wags on the tail section, as if to say, "Oh. Did you say something? Gosh, I guess we didn't hear."

"I'm fixing to sing a song."

With great effort, I shifted my tail section into Oh-Boy Wags. Over to my right, Drover fluttered his stub tail, and we both molded our faces into an expression we call Devoted Doggie.

Slim darted back into the house and returned with his five-string banjo. Like it or not, we were fixing to hear his song.

CHAPTER THREE

Slim Sits on the Porch in His Shorts

Did I mention that Slim had bought a banjo and was learning to play? It's true, and it came about because his lady friend, Miss Viola, had bought herself a mandolin and thought it would be fun if they got together once in a while and played music.

Viola was a pretty good musician. Slim was ... how can I say this? He tried, he really did, and sometimes it sounded okay, but he still had some work to do before he mastered the bluegrass style of picking.

Anyway, we crept back on the porch and Slim smiled. "That's better. Sit down." We sat. "Now, this is kind of a special occasion. It ain't often that I come up with a song this early in the morning."

I shot a glance at Drover. He was trying to be brave and so was I.

Slim continued. "Now, y'all pretend you're at Corn Eggly Hall in New York City. You're all dressed up, wearing tuxedos and black ties and them tall hats."

Oh brother.

"You're inside this huge auditorium, see, and it's jam-packed with people who've paid a hundred bucks apiece to hear the singing sensation from the Texas Panhandle."

This was so childish. I couldn't believe he was doing it.

He rose to his feet. "They turn off the house lights, and the place goes dark. A spotlight shines on the stage. Ten thousand people hold their breath, and I mean nobody says a word. Then . . ." —he extended his hand and raised it slowly—". . . the curtain rises and *there he is*! Slim Chance, the singing cowboy from Wolf Creek! He's wearing one of them coats like Porter Waggoner wears, with all that glitter-and-sparkle stuff. What do you call it?"

Could we get on with this?

"Spangles or jangles or sequins, stuff that glitters in the spotlight, see, and it tells you that this old boy didn't just fall off a truckload of turnips. He's a big star, and the place goes wild. They're

all on their feet, clapping their hands and yelling their heads off."

This was the wrong time to scratch a flea, but at that very moment I got drilled in the left armpit and HAD to do something about it. I cranked up my left hind leg and began hacking.

Slim beamed me a ferocious look. "Hey! Sit still and pay attention, we're coming to the good part."

Sorry.

"You've got no more manners than a goat."

I said I was sorry.

Slim returned to his little drama. "Okay, dogs, the audience claps and cheers for a whole minute, then the place gets quiet and everybody sits down. The Star looks out at the crowd and says, 'Thank you so very much, and now I'm going to sing y'all a song that comes straight from my heart. I wrote it myself, and I want to dedicate it to my momma back in Texas.'"

Oh brother!

And with that, Slim Chance sat down in his chair, put the banjo in his lap, and burst into song—wearing nothing but boxer shorts and a tee shirt, with nobody listening except a couple of dogs who couldn't escape. Here's the song, in case you're interested.

Sitting on the Porch in My Shorts

Sitting on the porch in my shorts.
Loafing outside in my underwear.
Sitting on the porch in my shorts.
Who'd want to be anywhere else but here?

A man's home is his castle, where he goes to
    escape the stress
Of a steady job and a gripey boss and fixing
    another mess on the ranch.
A job's okay if you do it right and don't get
    carried away.
When it's time to loaf, be serious about it, get
    started early in the day.

Sitting on the porch in my shorts.
Loafing outside in my underwear.
Sitting on the porch in my shorts.
Who'd want to be anywhere else but here?

If I was Commodore Vanderbilt, with all that
    railroad stock,
Do you suppose I'd grab a hammer and go to
    busting rock?
Heck no, I'd be on the porch of the Biltmore,
    listening to the frogs,
Getting a tan on my skinny legs and singing
    to my dogs. I'd sing . . .

Sitting on the porch in my shorts.
Loafing outside in my underwear.
Sitting on the porch in my shorts.
Who'd want to be anywhere else but here?

Sitting on the porch in my shorts.
Loafing outside in my underwear.
Sitting on the porch in my shorts.
Who'd want to be anywhere else?

Who'd want to be anywhere else?
I'd want to be right here.

Can you believe a grown man would do such a thing? I thought it was very strange, but I learned long ago to keep my opinions to myself. These people don't want to know what their dogs think—about music or anything else. We do what we have to do to keep our jobs, and sometimes that can be pretty embarrassing.

But there was a funny part to the story. See, old Slim thought he was all alone in the world, performing a ridiculous little song two miles from the nearest human.

Heh heh. Foolish man. See, halfway through the song, I heard a vehicle pull up behind his house, then the slam of a car door. Old Slim was onstage in New York City and didn't hear a thing.

And he didn't see the visitor coming up to the house. I did. I could have barked a warning but decided . . . why bother? If these people don't want to listen to their dogs, by George they can live with the consequences.

You want to guess who it was? Heh heh. Chief Deputy Bobby Kile from the Ochiltree County Sheriff's Department, a very important man. If you were going to make a fool of yourself, you might not want to do it in front of a deputy sheriff.

He approached the house. When he saw what was going on, he stopped and listened to the song. His face showed about what you'd expect. He couldn't believe what he was seeing and hearing. Then a nasty little smile slithered across his mouth, and he sneaked back to his car.

Now it gets really funny. When Slim finished his song, he smiled at us dogs, took a bow, and said, "What do you think about that, huh? Ain't that about the cutest little song you ever . . ."

At that very moment, the silence was shattered by the loud scream of a police siren.

You talk about SHOCKED. Slim Chance looked as though he'd backed into an electric fence. All the blood drained out of his face, and his eyes popped wide open. He whirled around and saw a man in uniform approaching the house. At that point, a gurgling sound came out of his mouth. I think he said, "Good honk!"

When he recognized Deputy Kile, he slumped into his chair and stared straight ahead with glazed eyes. The deputy placed a booted foot on the porch, looked up at the sky, and said, "Morning, Slim." Slim said nothing. "Do you live like this all the time?"

Slim's gaze slid around to the sheriff. "Bobby, this ain't funny. You almost gave me a heart attack with that si-reen."

The deputy laughed for a solid minute, while Slim's face turned a deep shade of red. At last he was able to speak. "Sorry. I couldn't resist." He went into another sputtering fit of laughter. He staggered up on the porch and fell into a chair beside Slim's.

Slim gave him a sour look. "Well, I hope you enjoyed it. You just about ruined my whole week."

"Were you singing to the dogs?"

Slim pulled himself into a stiff pose. "I certainly was, and it ain't the first time either. By grabs, this is America and if a man wants to sing to his dogs, he can do it."

The deputy nodded, still smiling.

"Every patriotic American ought to sit around in his underwear on the Fourth of July and sing to his dogs. It helps to remind us why we fought that war with the British."

"I thought it had something to do with taxation."

"Well, that was part of it, but the big thing was a man's right to walk around his own house in his shorts . . ."—Slim blistered the deputy with his eyes—". . . without some busybody from town sneaking up and blowing a frazzling si-reen!"

Deputy Kile laughed. "Are you through?"

"For now."

"Are you ready to listen to something?"

"I think that si-reen damaged my ears."

"Well, listen anyway." The deputy's smile faded into a serious expression. "Two days ago, a man walked into the grocery store in Twitchell. He had a pet skunk on a leash and was carrying a paper sack. He walked up to the cashier and handed her a note that said, 'Give me five pounds of baloney, or my skunk will spray your store.'"

Slim stared at him. "Is this a joke?"

The deputy shook his head. "Nope. But the cashier figured it was a joke. When he didn't leave, she tried to call the police." The deputy glanced around. "You got any more of that coffee?"

"No. Hurry up and finish the story. You've got me curious."

"I take it with cream and sugar."

Slim rose from his chair and growled, "You always was a tiresome man." Still holding his banjo, he hurried into the house (that was something new for Slim, hurrying) and returned minutes later, without the banjo, wearing a bathrobe, and holding a mug of coffee.

Deputy Kile nodded his thanks and looked into the cup. "Where's the cream and sugar?"

Slim flopped down in his chair. "The milk cow's been sick, and we had a crop failure on the sugarcane. Finish your story. I'm dying to hear this."

The deputy took a sip of coffee and flinched. "Is this coffee or mop water?"

"It's cowboy coffee, and you don't have to drink it. What happened in the store?"

The deputy took another sip, made an ugly face, and went on with the story. Wait till you hear this. You won't believe it.

CHAPTER FOUR

The Robber

If you recall, Chief Deputy Kile was telling Slim about a robbery in Twitchell. Here's the rest of the story.

"The man wasn't bluffing, and the skunk wasn't de-skunked. When the cashier reached for the phone, the man blew a high-pitched whistle. The skunk hopped up on its front legs, fanned out its tail, and fired."

Slim's face fell into a scowl. "Wait a second, I cain't believe this. You're telling me that he'd trained a skunk to spray on command?"

The deputy gave his head a solemn nod.

"I never heard of such a thing."

"Well, you can believe it or not, I don't care."

Slim pulled on his chin. "He blew a whistle and the skunk sprayed?"

The deputy nodded. "That's right, and as you might guess, skunks aren't good for grocery stores. Bad. They had to shut down for the day."

"Well, what happened to the crook?"

"He pulled a gas mask out of the paper sack and put it on his face. In all the excitement, he just walked away. Nobody had any idea who he was or where he went. He didn't get the baloney, but he just about ruined the store. The manager wants his scalp . . . yesterday."

Slim smirked. "If you catch the guy, what'll you charge him with? Attempted robbery with a skunk?"

The deputy laughed. "I'm not sure how we'll handle the charges, but we'll try to throw the book at him for property damage. It was pretty funny, but not cheap."

Slim leaned back in his chair, deep in thought. "So a man tries to rob a store in Twitchell with a skunk . . . and you're sitting on my porch, telling me about it. Is there a connection?"

The deputy rose from his chair and walked over to the edge of the porch. He pointed to some greenery below the porch. "Are those weeds or flowers?"

"Weeds. I've got plenty of 'em."

The deputy poured his coffee onto the weeds. "You don't have as many as you thought. This stuff ought to kill 'em dead."

He returned to his chair and pulled a piece of paper out of his shirt pocket. It was a map. He unfolded it and showed it to Slim.

"The day after that deal at the store, a rancher in Lipscomb County reported that somebody entered his house and stole some beef out of the deep freeze. The next day, another rancher up the creek made the same complaint, only this time the missing items were cans of food. Next day, same thing ... here, here, and here." He tapped his finger on the map, three times.

Slim squinted at the map. "Huh. It seems to be moving this way."

"That's right. I've got a hunch the crook's on foot in this empty ranch country and he's living off the land. He seems to be moving east, down the creek, and I guess he's got that skunk on a leash. If he sticks with the pattern, he's liable to show up around here."

Slim's eyebrows rose. "Huh. Well, thanks for the tip. I'll keep my eyes open."

The deputy's expression darkened and he lowered his voice. "Slim, if he shows up at your door, here's what I want you to do. Give him a cup of your coffee and call an ambulance. If he survives, I'll throw him in jail."

Cackling at his own joke, Deputy Kile started walking toward his car. Slim turned around in his chair and said, "Bobby, you ain't near as funny as you think."

The deputy waved. "Seriously, keep your eyes peeled and call if you see anything suspicious."

Slim cupped his hand around his mouth and yelled, "We'll probably have a lawsuit over you blowing my ears out with that si-reen. My lawyer'll be in touch."

The deputy climbed into his car, blew the siren one last time, and drove away. Slim settled back into his chair and looked down at us dogs. "He's too fussy to be an officer of the law." He took a gulp of coffee and spit out some grounds. "You know, he's got a point. This ain't my best . . ."

He didn't finish his sentence because, at that very moment, the telephone rang inside the house. He heard it but didn't move. Instead, he waved a hand in the air and growled, "I ain't going to answer it. I don't care who you are." The phone kept ringing. Slim dropped into his chair and crossed his arms over his chest. "I ain't a slave to the telephone. Go ahead and ring all you want."

Well, that was okay with me. The ringing stopped, and I stretched out on the porch and prepared for a nice little—the phone started ringing again. I sat up and threw a glance at Slim.

He heaved a sigh. "It's Loper. He knows I'm here and he won't quit." He pushed himself out of the chair and headed for the door.

Drover and I sprang to our feet and followed him. I mean, it was pretty obvious that he needed some help from the Security Division, and by George, we were glad to do it.

Slim had his mind on other things and didn't hold the screen door open for us, but we got there double-quick and managed to squirt through the opening, before the door slammed shut.

He stomped across the living room in his bare feet and snatched up the phone.

"Hello. Yes. I figured it was you. Because I couldn't think of anyone I wanted to talk to, and I still can't. What? Well, I'd planned to spend the whole day loafing on the porch, if you want to know the truth. But thanks for the invite. Bye."

He hung up the phone and turned to us dogs. "Loper and Sally May are having a Fourth of July picnic."

Picnic? Hey, great news!

"I ain't going. Too much trouble."

He headed for the porch again, so we had to do another scramble to make it through the screen door before it slammed shut. This time he noticed and said, "Are y'all following me around?"

Well, yes. That's what dogs do. If we'd been ordinary lazy mutts, we wouldn't have gone to the trouble. He was a lucky man to have dogs who cared about him.

He flopped down in his chair. "Well, now we can get back to the good life." He propped his feet on the banister and sang the chorus of his song:

> Sitting on the porch in my shorts.
> Loafing outside in my underwear.
> Sitting on the porch in my shorts.
> Who'd want to be anywhere else but here?

Yes sir, here was a happy man, doing the thing he did best and loved most (loaf), and he must have sat there for an hour or more. The sun rose above the trees along the creek. The temperature climbed, and flies buzzed around our ears. Drover and I found it harder and harder to keep our eyes open and finally we . . . dribbled off to slip . . . zzzzz.

I was awakened by the sound of Slim's voice. "You know, this ain't as much fun as I thought. In fact, it's kind of boring."

Drover and I blinked our eyes and yawned. Good point. I hadn't wanted to say anything but, yes, spending time on the porch with Slim wasn't exactly an electric experience.

He rose from the chair. "By netties, I think I'll go to the picnic. And I'll even take a bath." He headed for the front door. Drover and I leaped to our feet and fell in step behind him. He went through the screen door and pulled it shut. Looking back at us through the screen, he said, "Quit following me around. You're getting on my nerves." He vanished inside the house.

I turned to Drover. "We get on his nerves? Is that the thanks we get for being loyal dogs?"

A quiver came into Drover's voice. "Yeah, it's not our fault that he makes bad coffee."

"Exactly, but you know who always gets blamed. The dogs. This has been going on for years, Drover, and sometimes I wonder why we put up with it. If these people had to live a day without dogs, maybe they'd appreciate all the things we do."

"Yeah, we ought to run away from home."

"Maybe we should."

"That would teach him."

"It really would. What do you think, should we walk off the job and let him learn the hard way?"

"Yeah, let's do. It would serve him right."

"Then it's settled. We're going on strike!"

We left the porch and marched down the side-walk, the first leg of a long journey that would take us we-knew-not-where. When we reached the yard gate, Drover stopped and glanced around. "But you know, it's kind of hot."

"It is, isn't it?"

"Yeah. Maybe we ought to wait for a cooler day."

I gave that some thought. "It might be better to wait."

"Yeah. You know, October will be here before you know it."

"Exactly. Okay, we'll let him off the hook this time." We marched back to the porch and flopped down. "Slim has no idea how close he came to los-ing the entire Security Division."

"Yeah, he took a chance, leaving us out here in this heat." Drover was silent for a moment. "Reckon it's cooler in the house?"

"Oh sure."

"Why don't we go inside?"

I stared at the runt. "Because we can't. He shut us out. He doesn't want to share his house."

A grin spread across his mouth. "Yeah, but I know a trick."

I couldn't imagine what "trick" he had in mind.

In fact, if he'd learned a trick, it would be the biggest news of the week. I followed him over to the screen door and watched.

He hooked his left front paw under the bottom of the screen door and gave it a jerk. The door opened wide enough for him to scoot through the crack. Inside the house, he grinned at me through the screen. "What do you think?"

It took me a moment to recover from the shock. "When did you learn to do that?"

"Oh, a couple of weeks ago. I've been practicing."

"It didn't look all that difficult. I mean, you just hooked your claws under the door and pulled, right?"

"Yeah, any dog could do it."

"Exactly my point. Stand back, I'm coming in."

And with that . . . well, you'll see. It wasn't as easy as you might think.

Slim Goes to
the Picnic

I marched up to the door, hooked the claws of my left front paw under the bottom, and gave it a...

BONK!

On the other side of the screen, Drover shook his head. "No, it works better if you keep your face out of the way."

Rubbing my nose, I glared at him through the screen door. "Drover, please don't dwell on the obvious. That was just a practice run. Watch this." I hooked my paw under the bottom of the door and gave it a mighty...

BONK!

Drover shook his head again. "No, you have to move your nose out of the way."

"Don't tell me what to do! It's a stupid door, that's all. Stand back."

BONK!

My nose ached, my eyes watered, and for a moment of heartbeats, I thought about ripping the door right off its hinges. I mean, this was the most frustrating . . . I took several deep breaths and tried to calm my savage instincts. "Okay, I've got a better idea. You open it."

"Well, I don't think I can."

"Of course you can. You already did it once."

"Yeah, but that was out on the porch. Everything's backward when you do it inside. See, if you pull from the inside, it makes the door close."

"Then *push*. Had you thought of that? If everything's backward, then do the opposite of what you did before."

He rolled his eyes around. "Well . . . the opposite of a door is a window, and I don't think I can open a window."

"Drover, I am your commanding officer, and I'm getting hot out here. Push the door and let me in!" Poof. The little dunce vanished before my very eyes. "Drover, come back! Do you hear me?" I cocked my ear and listened. Not a sound. "Drover, come back here and open this door!"

I could hear Slim singing in the bathtub but not a sound from little Mister Sneak in the House. I decided to try a softer approach.

"All right, Drover, you've had your little moment of rebellion, and I'm sure you enjoyed it. Now it's time to get this thing resolved and move on with our lives." He didn't come, so I screamed, "Drover, if you don't report to the front door on the count of three, you will be court-martialed and fed to the buzzards! One! Two! Three!"

I narrowed my eyes and peered through the screen. Nothing. Well, the disobedient little wretch had left me no choice. I gave the door three stern barks, marched away in triumph, and finished my nap on the porch.

Like I said, it was a stupid door, and there isn't much we can do with ... phooey.

I had a great nap, and Slim must have had a great bath. He wasn't the kind of man who craved bathwater very often, but once he got there, he stayed for a while. I don't know if he had rubber ducks and toy boats in there, but something kept him occupied.

Oh yes, his singing. He sang every song ever recorded by Slim Whitman, Bob Wills, and Patsy Cline. Fortunately, I was able to sleep through most of it and was finally awakened by the sound of him tromping around inside the house. I rushed to the screen door, sat down facing the house, and went into the pose we call I've Been Waiting for Hours.

He came to the door and saw me. My goodness, he had been transformed. He'd washed and combed his hair. He'd put on a clean shirt, a fresh pair of jeans, a shiny pair of go-to-town boots, and a new straw hat. He said, "Have you been there all this time?"

Oh yes, no question about it. That's a dog's lot in life, waiting for his people.

"Well, what do you think?" He grinned and twirled around, as though he were ... I don't know, modeling his clothes, I guess. "Old Slim cleans up pretty good, don't he? Heh. Miss Viola might be at the picnic, see, and a man wants to look his best." His grin faded. "Say, when I left, there was two of you yardbirds out there. Where's Stub Tail?"

I gave him a look that said, "We dogs never rat on a friend, but ... HE WEASELED HIS WAY INTO YOUR HOUSE!"

Slim's face fell into a pile of wrinkles, and he muttered, "I wonder ..." He disappeared inside the house, then I heard his voice. "Get out from under that bed! Hyah, scat!" Moments later, Drover came flying out the door, and I began roasting him with Glares of Rebuke.

He lowered his head and tail and sniffled. "Gosh, what did I do?"

I marched over to him. "Breaking and entering, insubordination, disobeying an order, abandoning a comrade, and hiding under a bed without permission. Oh, and showing off in front of a superior officer."

"Yeah, but I wasn't trying to show off, honest."

"Well, you did. Not only did you open the door all by yourself, but you stood there and watched while your commanding officer tried the same trick three times and *failed*! How do you suppose that affects the morale of this unit?"

"Well, I didn't think of that."

"No, because you're a selfish little creep. Drover, we ought to throw the book at you."

"I thought it was a pretty good trick."

"Of course it was a good trick and that's the whole point. You can do bad tricks all day, and nobody will care. It's the good ones that cause the damage."

He hung his head. "Sorry."

"Are you really sorry? Is this coming from your heart?"

He grinned. "Not really."

"That's what I thought. Stand with your nose in the corner, now! Move!"

He glanced around. "Well, there's no corner on a porch."

I moved my gaze around the porch. Hmm. He had a point. "Okay, then stand with your nose against the house. Move it!"

He moaned and whined, but I didn't care. My heart had turned to stone. By George, if we don't take the time to teach the underlings how to act, they'll run wild and before you know it . . . something . . . everything will go to blazes.

I don't enjoy being hard on the men, but you can't run a Security Division without order, discipline, and respect.

He stood with his nose against the house and I sat in front of the door, waiting for Slim to emerge. Moments later, he came breezing out the . . . BAM!

"Out of the way, Bozo, I've got places to go."

What was the deal with that door? Did it hate dogs? Four times in the past hour, it had struck me for no good reason and I was about ready to . . . oh well, justice would have to wait. Slim had invited us to a picnic.

Okay, he hadn't exactly invited us, but I was pretty sure that he wanted us to go. What's a picnic without dogs, right?

I turned to the jailbird. "All right, Drover, I'm going to let you out on parole, but one more mistake and you'll be right back in the brig."

His face bloomed into a smile. "Oh goodie, so I'm a free dog?"

We trotted out the yard gate. "For now, yes, and hurry up. Slim's waiting to take us . . ." The pickup drove away from the house. I was stunned. "What? He's leaving without us? Surely there's been a mistake."

"Maybe he just went to the mailbox."

I gave that some thought. "Of course, why didn't I think of that? He's gone to check the mail, and he'll be right back."

We sat down and waited. And waited. Then Drover said, "You know what? I don't think he's coming back."

"Don't be ridiculous. He wouldn't dare . . ." At that moment, my keen eyes caught a flash of movement down at the saddle shed. I turned my head and took a closer look. "Oh, there he is down at the shed. See?"

Drover squinted toward the shed. "Oh yeah, there he is. I guess you were right, he came back for us."

"Heh. I know him pretty well, Drover. He'll

bluster and threaten, but when it's time to go to a picnic, he'll want to take his dogs."

"I wonder what he did with the pickup."

"The pickup?"

"Yeah, when he left, he was driving a pickup. I don't see it now."

I turned my Visual Scanners toward the north and adjusted the focus. A man had just come out of the little wooden shed where Slim kept his saddle and horse feed. "Good point, son. I don't see his pickup either, so let's do a little detective work here."

"Oh boy, this'll be fun."

"He drove up to the county road to check the mail, and the pickup quit on him."

Drover nodded. "Yeah, and he had to walk back from the mailbox."

"Exactly. He's always talking about how his pickup is a piece of junk."

"Yeah, and now he'll have to walk to the picnic. Boy, he'll be mad about . . ." Drover narrowed his eyes. "I didn't know he was wearing a baseball cap."

"He wasn't. In fact, he was wearing a brand-new straw hat."

"Well, he's wearing a cap now."

"Impossible." I gave the man a closer look. He

was walking toward the house. "Hmmm. Now that's strange. He's wearing a cap. Okay, let's see if we can figure this out. He decided that a straw hat would be too hot, so he changed to a cap."

"Yeah, and you know what else? He changed his clothes, too."

"Rubbish. He would never go to all that trouble." I studied the man. "Hmmm. Okay, here's our next clue. He changed his clothes, and we don't know why."

"Yeah, but ..." All at once, the runt edged around behind me. "Hank, I don't think that's Slim."

"What? Drover, sometimes you come up with the craziest notions. Of course it's Slim. Who else ..." I studied the man again. Huh? "Drover, I don't want to alarm you, but *that's not Slim*."

"Yeah, that's what I said."

"Don't argue with me. That's not Slim. He's too short and he's got long hair and . . ." I, uh, moved around behind Drover. "Soldier, we've got a stranger on the place. Maybe you'd better trot down there and give him a bark. What do you think?"

He gave me a blank stare. "Me! Are you crazy? You're the Head of Ranch Security."

"Well, sure, but ..." My mind was racing. "Okay, here's the plan. We'll pull all our troops back to the porch and set up a line of defense. If he leaves, we won't bark. If he tries to enter the house, we'll hit him with everything we've got. What do you think?"

Zoom! Drover was already streaking toward the porch like a little comet, leaving me out in front of the house without reserves. I wheeled around, hit Turbo Four, and made a dash for the porch.

When I got there, Drover was huddled behind Slim's chair. "Coward! Get out from behind that chair." He didn't move, so I did what any normal American dog would have done. I pushed and shoved and joined him behind the chair.

There, in our foxhole on the front lines, we huddled together and listened to the sound of the stranger's footsteps. *He was coming toward the house!*

A Mysterious
Visitor

~~~~~~

A re you scared? Good, because I was, too. Any
dog would have been scared. I mean, Slim's
house was twenty-five miles from the nearest
town, so far out in the country that on a clear day,
you could see boondocks in the distance. The place
was so isolated that Slim could sit out on the
porch in his underwear and sing corny songs.

Yet a stranger had just appeared and was coming toward the house!

So, yes, I was scared and I'm not ashamed to
admit it. But Drover was in worse shape. He was
so scared, his teeth were clicking together. "Drover,
try to be professional . . . and stop clicking your
teeth."

"I c-c-can't help it."

"Of course you can. Put a gag in your mouth."
You know what he did? He covered his eyes with
his paws. "Drover, those are your eyes, not your
mouth!"

"Yeah, but if I don't see anything, maybe I won't
be so scared."

"All right, give it a try."

I turned my gaze back to the stranger. He
walked up to the yard gate and stopped. That
gave me enough time to scan his face and run it
through Data Control's huge database of faces.
It came back negative. Nobody in our Security
Division had ever seen this guy before.

He glanced around and called out, "Hello!
Anybody home?"

Drover began to twitch and squirm. "Should
we tell him we're here?"

"Shhh! Absolutely not. We might need the element of surprise."

"I need the element of courage."

"Maybe he'll leave. Shhh."

The man called out again. "I'm from the electric company. I need to take a reading on your meter. Hello?"

I almost fainted with relief. "It's okay, son.
He's reading meters. They do it every month."

"If he works for the power company, how come he's not wearing a uniform?"

"Because...look, maybe it was dirty. Aren't you glad he didn't come out here in a dirty shirt?"

"I don't care. I don't like his looks."

"Drover, you're being weird. He's just doing his job, and we might as well be friendly. Let's step out and say hello."

"Got it. I'll be right behind you."

For the record, let me point out that Drover not only stayed "right behind" me, he stayed right behind the chair. In other words, he didn't move, and I had to greet the meter man all by myself.

I stepped out from behind the chair and waved my tail back and forth. He saw me and smiled. "Oh, there you are. I figured you were around somewhere. I'm Leland. You remember me?"

Uh...no.

"You don't? Shucks, I come down here every month." He came through the gate and walked up to the porch steps. There, he stopped. "You remember me now?"

Well . . . okay, maybe. My memory was a little hazy.

He motioned with his fingers. "Come here and I'll give you some sugar."

I crept toward him, and he began rubbing me behind the ears. They were good rubs. I was liking this guy better all the time. Then he started scratching me along the backbone, ha ha, and I guess you know what that does. All at once my right hind leg coiled up and started pumping.

It's kind of mysterious, how that happens, and I can't say that I understand it, but people who know dogs can do it and it's really fun. He scratched and I pumped, and we had definitely become good pals.

He laughed and gave me a pat on the ribs. "Well, I'd better get back to work. I'll step inside the house, read the meter, and get on my way. It's kind of a bummer to work on a holiday, but that's my job."

Yes, I understood about working on holidays. I had one of those jobs myself: never a day off, never a moment's rest. It was a hard life and we had to take our little pleasures where we could find them, mostly in the pride that came from doing the job right.

My new friend walked up the steps and went inside the house. I marched over to the chair and glared down at my ... whatever he was, my assistant who never seemed to get around to assisting.

"Well, what do you say now?"

"He's wearing a wrinkled shirt."

"How can you say that?"

"'Cause I saw it. It looks like he slept in it."

"Oh brother! You're going to hold that against him? Look, he's a working man. Those of us who work get dirty and wrinkled. You ought to try it sometime."

"He's got snake eyes. I don't trust him."

"Drover, you are the most . . . snake eyes! I can't believe you said that."

We heard noise coming from inside the house and naturally Drover had to make a big deal out of it. "If he's checking meters, how come he's making so much noise?"

"Because . . . because meters are sometimes hard to find."

"Yeah, but it's on a power pole beside the barn."

"Well, there you are. He's trying to find it."

Drover rolled his gaze around. "But if he's a meter man, how come he doesn't know where the meter is?"

I stared into the vacuum of his eyes. "Drover, that is one of the dumbest questions you've ever asked. The poor man has to work on a holiday, and all you can do is . . ."

At that moment, the door opened and Leland

stepped outside. Hmmm. That was odd. He seemed to be carrying several packages of ... was that frozen beef?

He beamed us a smile. "Say, you're getting low amperage and the deep freeze ain't working right. I'm going to take some of this meat back to the office and put it in cold storage. Otherwise, it's liable to spoil in this heat." He started down the porch steps. "I'll call your master in the morning and explain everything. Y'all have a good day."

He walked with rapid steps down the sidewalk and out the gate.

I whirled around to Drover. "Snake eyes, huh? Drover, I'm ashamed of you."

He was staring straight ahead and whispered, "Hank, do you remember what the deputy said?"

"Deputy? What deputy? Oh, him. Of course I do. He said that Slim looked ridiculous, sitting out on the porch in his drawers. And you know what? He was right."

"No, I mean ... about the man who tried to rob the store?"

Huh?

It hit me like a cinderblock falling out of the sky. All at once my mind was reeling' and I thought I might faint. "Holy drokes, Smoker, do you remember what the deputy said?"

"The robber steals food out of ranch houses."

"Right, exactly." I paced a few steps away and tried to control the whirlwind inside my head. "Drover, if the electric meter is on a power pole, why did he need to go inside the house?"

"Well, I wondered about that."

"And why would a meter man walk out of a house with an armload of frozen beef?"

"I guess he doesn't like canned mackerel."

I whirled around and faced my assistant. "Don't you get it? He's no more a meter man than I am. He's a crook, and he stole food right under our noses!"

"I think it was your nose."

I began pacing back and forth. Thoughts, clues, and ideas were pouring through my mind like a raging river. "Drover, something about that guy told me not to trust him."

"Yeah, the snake eyes."

"He had snake eyes, did you notice? And he was wearing a wrinkled shirt, and he had long stringy hair."

"Yeah, I tried to tell you."

I marched over to him and stuck my nose in his face. "If you tried so hard to tell me, then why didn't you tell me?"

"Because you never listen."

For a moment of heartbeats, I thought I might explode right there in his face, but a voice inside my head told me to be mature. "Drover, I'm going to pretend that I didn't hear that, but if it happens again, I'll have to put it in my report."

"Thanks. What are we going to do now?"

"That's a great question, and I'm glad you asked." I laid a paw across his shoulder. "Drover, when Slim figures out that somebody walked into his house and stole beef, he's going to throw a hissy fit."

"Yeah, he'll probably blame it on us."

"Exactly. It would smear the reputations of all of us in the Security Division. Why, it might take us years to win back his trust. But I think there's a way out of this."

"There is?"

"Yes, and the really good part is that it could give your career a boost."

"Gosh, no fooling?"

"Honest, and I mean a BIG boost—stripes, stars, medals, commendations, the whole nine yards of career-enhancing so-forths. I mean, this could put you on an elevator to the top."

"I'll be derned. What would I have to do?"

"Well, that's the best part: not much. Just sneak up behind the crook, bite him on the hip pocket, and then bark like you're the baddest dog in five Texas counties. What do you think?"

To my complete amazement, the runt narrowed his eyes into cruel slits and began rolling the muscles in his shoulders. "You know, I think I can do it!"

"That's the spirit! Now tell me, who's the baddest dog in five Texas counties?"

"Me!"

"Who's going to protect this ranch?"

He started jumping up and down. "Me!"

"Are you mad enough?"

"Yeah!"

"Are you bad enough?"

"Oh yeah!"

"Can you do it?"

"I can do it!"

I whopped him on the back. "All right, soldier, go out there and take care of business. No prisoners!"

"No prisoners!"

And with that ... well, you'll have to keep reading to find out.

CHAPTER SEVEN

The Secret
Weapon

What a miracle! I had never seen this side of Drover and, well, it was pretty amazing. I mean, for years the little mutt had dodged every dangerous mission and avoided every kind of productive labor, but now . . .

You know, when you see this kind of attitude change in the troops, you have to chalk it up to . . . well, great leadership. Don't let anyone kid you, it all starts at the top. If you've got the right kind of leadership at the top, by George, it filters down through the ranks and you can see it in the performance of the men.

I don't want to take too much of the credit, but we need to be honest. Drover's fighting spirit didn't come out of a can of chopped liver. And I was SO PROUD of the little mutt, I was about to bust my buttons.

So there was my First Assistant, hopping up and down, throwing punches, and growling like . . . I don't know what. Like a second-string scrub who'd suddenly found the desire to go into the game and turn things around.

"All right, son, go out there and show us what you can do!"

In a burst of pure raw power, he tore away and . . . why was he going toward the house? And what . . .

Huh?

Okay, forget all that stuff about Drover's big change in attitude. Strike it from the record. It was a bogus report. Somebody was badly misquoted.

You know what the little mutter-mumble did? HE RAN TO THE DOOR, HOOKED HIS PAW UNDER THE BOTTOM, AND VANISHED INSIDE THE HOUSE!!

I was stunned, speechless. It took me a whole minute to find the voice of righteous anger.

"Drover, report to the front immediately!" I banged on the door. "Drover, come out of there, and that is a direct order!" Not a sound. No doubt he had already burrowed two miles deep under

Slim's bed. "All right, you little traitor, you will be court-martialed for this! If I ever get my paws on you . . ."

Gulp.

Now what? I whirled around and saw that the crook had almost reached the saddle shed. If someone didn't do something fast . . . well, the reputation of the Security Division would go down in flames, and we could say good-bye to our jobs, friends, nights in the house, free dog food, and all the other benefits we enjoyed as ranch employees.

There are times when a dog has to reach deep inside and grope around for something that resembles courage, and sometimes it's not easy to find. Like now. With all my heart and soul, I didn't want to do what I had to do, but it had to be done.

I filled my lungs with a big gulp of carbon diego, squared my enormous shoulders, and marched off to war. I passed through the gate and kept going. Outside the gate, I flipped several switches and raised Data Control on our Emergency Frequency.

"DC, we have the target in sight."

"Proceed to target and acquire."

"Target is acquired, and the signal is strong."

"Lock it into the computer."

"Computer is locked."

"Arm the weapon."

"The weapon is armed and ready. Request permission to fire."

"Roger that. Fire the weapon!"

In a burst of fire and smoke, I launched the weapon and went streaking toward the crosshairs on the enemy's left hip pocket. The thief suspected nothing, never saw me coming, and fellers, when I fitted my jaws around his pocket, he just sort of went off in all directions, and we're talking about arms flying and packages of frozen meat falling like hailstones.

Holding his bitten hiney, he whirled around and saw me for the first time. "You! Now, why'd you go and do that?"

I gave him a snarl that said, "Because you're a liar and a thief, and I don't like either one of those things. Get off my ranch and don't ever come back, or you'll get the rest of what I started."

Pretty impressive, huh? You bet. I didn't cut the guy any slack. When they push me over the line, they get no mercy.

What did he do? Heh heh. You'll love this. He raised his hands in the air and started edging toward the saddle shed. "All right, doggie, you've got the goods on me. I give up. Keep the meat. You won, fair and square, and I've got no hard feelings. In fact, I'm going to give you a prize."

A prize? How about that, huh? Wow, what a triumph! The creep darted inside the shed and ... what was that thing? A cat on a leash? Cats don't have black and white stripes, do they? Or long bushy tails?

Huh?

Oops. All at once I remembered the rest of the deputy's story, the part about the, uh, Secret Weapon. You'd probably forgotten all about it, but ...

A skunk. He brought his pet skunk out of the shed and pointed a finger directly at me. "Rosebud, that dog just said your momma's a skunk. Are you going to take that from a dog? Huh? No? Then git 'im!" He put a little plastic whistle between his lips and blew. TWEET!

Before I could think or move, Rosebud hopped up into firing position and sent a ball of something yellow rolling in my direction. It wasn't a ball of fire. It was something a whole lot ...

SPLAT!

... worse. We've talked about skunks, right? And all the damage they can do? Big damage, especially if they land a direct hit. This one did. I mean, it happened so fast ...

Boy, you talk about STINK! You talk about

toxic air and going blind and gasping for breath! Fellers, when you get ambushed by a skunk, you know you've been ambushed. I mean, this was the same little monster that had shut down a grocery store, and I promise, anything that can shut down a store can shut down a dog.

I staggered and stumbled through the cloud of poisonous yellow fog. "Hank to Drover, over. We have a dog down! Repeat, dog down, dog down! Activate all units, launch the second wave, send a chopper, help!"

You probably think Drover rushed out of the house and came to my rescue, right? Ha. What a joke. He didn't rush out of the house. He probably didn't even hear my distress call. Don't forget where he was hiding—under Slim's bed. There were so many spiderwebs under that bed, sound waves had no chance of getting there.

He didn't come to my rescue, and to be honest, even if he had, I don't know what he could have done. I mean, the damage had been done and I was WEARING it, because every cell and fiber of my body had been embalmed with skunk.

I staggered through the poisoned cloud and went straight into Skunk Countermeasures. Have we discussed SCM? Maybe not, because it's classified information and . . . well, we don't want our enemies to know how we deal with exotic weaponry such as your skunk attacks.

I'm sure you understand. See, Security Work is really a giant game of chess, played against adversaries who are clever beyond our wildest dreams. They would love to know our secret countermeasures for detoxifying a dog that has been seriously skunked, and if I revealed it here . . . well, they might intercept the message.

See, they're watching us all the time and listening to every word we say. They never sleep, never rest, never give up. The secret war goes on around the clock and we have to . . .

I guess it wouldn't hurt to reveal our secrets, because the terrible truth is that WE DON'T HAVE ANY SKUNK COUNTERMEASURES. When you get skunked, you're skunked, buddy, and you wear it until it falls off. The best you can do is roll around in some tall grass and try to figure out how to live with yourself for the next week.

The only good news about skunking is that it sort of melts the wiring in your nose and, after a while, you can't smell much of anything. That's not great news, but it beats nothing, right?

What happened to the crook and his Secret Weapon? Whilst I was choking and gasping and staggering through the yellow fog, they just walked away—probably laughing their heads off. They vanished without a trace.

Wait. They left one trace, a package of frozen hamburger. Once the fog had lifted and I was able to breathe again, I found the package in front of the saddle shed. You probably think that after such a terrible ordeal, I had no interest in collecting evidence or working up the case. Wrong.

See, most of your ordinary ranch mutts would have dropped the case right there, I mean, quit in shame and disgust. Not me, fellers. As I've said before, cowdogs are just a little bit special and for us, "quit" is a four-letter word.

Hmmm. You know what? It really is a four-letter word. Oh well.

Where were we? Oh yes, we cowdogs don't consider ourselves ordinary and we don't know how to quit. When the going gets tough, we get going. When the other dogs go to the house, we're still out there working the case. And when we find an important piece of evidence . . . well, sometimes we eat it.

Heh heh.

Why not? I hadn't stolen it out of Slim's deep freeze or left it in front of the barn. Out there in the hot sun it would spoil, so I did the only sensible thing and wolfed it down. Okay, there wasn't much "wolfing," because you can't "wolf" a block of frozen meat, but I sure as thunder chewed and hacked my way through it and, uh, sent it to the lab, shall we say.

It was delicious, best meal I'd had in months.

Burp.

And at that point, after collecting and cataloging the evidence and taking careful notes about the cream sign . . . the crime scene, that is . . . after taking measurements and photographs and careful notes about the cream sign, I was ready to move to the next stage of the investigation.

I had to get an urgent message to Slim that his deep freeze had been burgled, and I mean fast, before the crook and his Secret Weapon struck again.

Here, we encountered a problem: Slim wasn't around to be warned. He had left the premises and was attending a picnic at Loper and Sally May's place, two miles up the creek. In other words, I would have to run two miles in the blazing heat of July.

Could I handle the job? You bet. A lot of your ordinary mutts would say, "Forget this," and retire to a shady spot beneath some trees. Not me.

I taxied into the wind, made one last check of the instruments, closed the canopy, and pushed the throttle all the way up to Turbo Six.

Within seconds, I leveled off at thirty thousand feet, trimmed the flaps, and pulled the throttle back to cruising speed. Looking down at the Earth below, I heard a voice inside my head. It said, "It's really hot out here, and two miles is a long way. Forget this."

I wasn't sure whose voice I'd heard, but suddenly it hit me that ... the voice was right! A dog has no business running around in brutal heat. It's very dangerous. Why, dogs have been known to faint, collapse, and even perish while jogging in the heat, and who needs that?

I felt sure that if Slim had been there beside me, he would have begged me to scuttle the mission, pointing out the obvious—that if anything happened to me, the ranch would just ... well, fall apart.

As much as I hated to do it, I cut the engines, went gliding down through the cloudosphere, and executed a smooth landing on the county road beside the mailbox.

With a heavy heart, I climbed out of the cockpit, hurried to the shade of the nearest tree, and flopped down. There, I began pumping fresh air across my dripping tongue and went into a routine we call Maybe Next Time.

After ten minutes of this, I checked gauges and was glad to see that all my precious bodily fluids had returned to their normal readings. Would I plunge on with the mission? No way. That piece of shade had my name written all over it and I planned to ...

Huh?

I heard footsteps approaching. It was the robber ... *and he was coming back to finish me off!*

False Alarm

Okay, relax. It was Drover, chugging down the dusty road and coming in my direction. Oh brother. Was there anyone I would rather NOT see at that particular moment? No. I flattened myself out on the ground and tried to melt into the shadows.

Maybe he would go right past and never see me.

He trotted up to the mailbox and stopped, glanced around, and called out, "Hank? Where'd you go? Listen, I'm feeling kind of guilty about being such a little chicken. Terrible guilt, honest, and I've decided to start my life all over again. Hello?"

I held my breath and didn't make a sound. He

heaved a sigh and started out again, trotting west on the county road and heading toward Ranch Headquarters. He didn't see me, and that was great.

But then he stopped and sniffed the air. He turned around and looked straight at me. His face bloomed into a smile. "Oh, hi. There for a second, I thought I smelled a skunk." He came skipping toward me, then skidded to a stop. He sniffed the air again. "I did smell a skunk. Oh my gosh, is that . . . you?"

"It's me, and let's go straight to the point. You're fired. Clean out your desk, turn in your badge, and disappear. I never want to speak to you again. Good-bye."

"You mean . . ."

"I mean it's over. I gave you every chance in the world to make something of yourself. Instead, you made a mess of everything."

He hung his head. "I know but I can't help it. I'm such a chicken!" He broke down and started crying. "Sometimes I can't stand myself, but I'm all I've got."

"Yeah, well, that's real bad luck."

"I promised Mom that I'd be a good little dog . . . and now I'll have to tell her that I got fired! It'll just break her heart!"

What can you say? I'm pretty hard-boiled (you have to be in my line of work), but this was no fun.

"Hank, give me just . . . five more chances."

"Absolutely not."

He bawled some more. "Give me just . . . three more chances."

"No! I've made my decision, and there's no turning back. Sorry."

More bawling and squawling, then he moaned, "Okay, one last chance, that's all, just one."

He boo-hooed for another minute, while I reviewed his file and counted the plink of his tears on the ground. (Twelve). At last I couldn't stand any more of it. "All right, quit bawling. One more chance, but you have to take the Pledge of No Chicken. Stand at attention, raise your right paw, and repeat the Pledge."

He dried his eyes, snapped to attention, and raised his paw. "Yeah, but I don't remember it."

"I haven't given it yet."

"Oh. Sorry."

"Here's the Pledge, so pay attention. 'I, Drover C. Dog, do solomonly swear to be brave and bold, to stop being a chickenhearted little mutt, and never the twang shall meet."

"What's a twang?"

"Say the Pledge!"

He said the words, and I began pacing in front of him. "All right, trooper, you're back on the force. I'm taking a huge career risk, so don't blow it. Here's your first assignment." I gave him a brief account of my scuffle with the burglar and his skunk. "I'm sending you up to headquarters to warn Slim. Can you handle that?"

"Oh, that's why you stink so bad?"

I leaned down into his face. "Can you handle the job or not?"

He coughed and fanned the air in front of his face. "Oh yeah, I can do it, 'cause I took the Pledge of No Chicken."

"Good. I'll set up a command post over there in the shade and wait for your report."

He began hopping up and down. "Oh, this'll be fun!"

"Drover, it won't be fun. It's hotter than a depot stove."

"Yeah, but Beulah might be at the picnic. Bye now, here I go!"

He went skipping down the road like a little . . . I don't know what. Like a happy little grasshopper, I suppose.

"Drover, halt! Come back here!"

He came back and gave me a puzzled look. "Gosh, did I do something wrong?"

"Not yet. We've had a change of odors."

"Yeah, I noticed."

"I said, we've had a change of *orders*. I'm going with you."

"But I thought ..."

"In this heat, the trip to headquarters could be dangerous. You just rejoined the force five minutes ago, and we'd hate for anything bad to happen."

"Gosh, that's nice."

"Let's move out."

I began marching down the middle of the road. Drover followed along behind—just where he belonged. After a moment, he said, "Oh, I get it now. Beulah."

"That's right, pal. She's mine, and don't you even speak to her."

"She won't like your smell."

"She'll love my smell. Women go for a deep manly aroma."

"Yeah, but you tried that once and it backfired."

"Drover, when I need your advice about romance, I'll ask for it. In the meantime, please keep your trap shut."

"You never learn."

"I beg your pardon?"

"Nothing. I was just shutting my trap."

As I predicted, it was a long hot trip to headquarters. We had to stop twice to rest in the shade, but thirty minutes later, we reached our destination. Even at a distance we could see that dozens of friends and neighbors had turned out for the picnic.

Several men in aprons cooked hamburgers on a big iron grill. A group of ladies sat in lawn chairs, talking and laughing, while another group played instruments and sang. Children were playing softball, and several ranchers slouched against trees, discussing grass and cattle. Others were pitching horseshoes.

As we marched toward the picnic ground, Drover said, "How are you going to tell Slim about the burglar?"

"I beg your pardon?"

"The message. We made the trip so you could warn Slim about the burglar. How do you say 'burglar' in Tailwag?"

"I don't know, but I'm sure you'll figure it out."

"Me! But I thought ..."

"I've decided to let you handle it, son."

"Yeah, but all I've got is a stub tail."

"Use a simple wig-wag procedure and double the speed. Wig-wig-wag-wag-wiggy-wiggle."

"That means 'hamburger.'"

I stopped and gazed into the emptiness of his eyes. "Drover, I'm going to be busy entertaining a certain lady dog. I don't have time to teach you how to communicate with the human race. Go to Slim and tell him about the burglar. Use your tiny mind and figure it out." I gave him a pat on the shoulder. "It's good to have you back on the force."

"Thanks."

"Since you're on probation, I know you won't bungle this assignment."

He began to wheeze. "You know, pressure really messes me up."

"Pressure is good for us, son. If it weren't for pressure, all the tires in this world would be flat."

"I don't get it."

"Air pressure. That's the difference between a tire that works and one that's flat. Do you want to spend your whole life as a flat tire?"

He wheezed again. "Boy, I sure could use some air."

"I'm sure you'll find some at the picnic. This air is filled with air. Now, run along and take care of business. I'll expect a full report in half an hour."

He whined and wheezed, but I didn't have time to hear his little complaints. I had bigger flies to fry. See, I had already searched the crowd and spotted . . . mercy! Have we discussed Miss Beulah the Collie? Yes, surely we have, because for years she had been the object of my dreams and devotion.

Flaxen hair. Dewberry eyes. Long collie ears and a long collie nose. A perfect tail, a perfect set of teeth, perfect toes . . . wow, what a woman!

How many nights had she visited me in my dreams? Dozens of times, hundreds of times. In my dreams, she belonged to me, and me alone, but the problem with dreams is that at sunrise, the show's over and then we have to deal with . . . well, facts.

See, there was a bird dog in her life. Plato. They stayed on the same ranch, down the creek from us, and she seemed to have some kind of weird affection for him. I had never understood that. I mean, in so many ways she seemed gifted and intelligent. How could she like a bird dog when she could have . . . well, ME for example?

It made no sense, none. As a group, bird dogs tend to be dull, boring, and dumber than dirt, and Plato was all of those things—times five. What can you say about a dog that spends his entire life sniffing the ground, chasing birds, fetching sticks, and pointing old tennis shoes?

What you can say is that he was exactly the

kind of mutt that Beulah should have avoided like a cloud of germs, but she didn't. She actually seemed to like the creep, even though I had tried every trick in the book to win her heart.

You know, a lot of dogs would have gotten discouraged and quit. Me? I often got discouraged but *didn't* quit. I would never quit! I would never give up hope that one day, the germ clouds would lift and she would see the Birdly Wonder for what he was—a stick-tailed buffoon who didn't deserve the time of day, much less her affection.

Those were the thoughts that echoed through the caverns of my mind as I went to my One and Only True Love. Yes, there she sat in the shade of an elm tree, watching all the activities that were going on at the picnic, taking it all in with her delicious brown eyes.

As I moved toward her through the crowd, I became aware of a very important detail. She was sitting alone! NO BIRD DOG. My heart leaped with joy. Holy smokes, maybe she had finally ditched the pest!

I quickened my pace and listened to the snare drum of my heart, beating out wild rhythms. Could this be the day? My heart said . . . yes!

Kangaroos Are
Marsh Soup Eels

Ten feet away from Miss Beulah, I stopped. I wanted to be subtitle about this, don't you see. Subtle. I wanted to be subtle.

A lot of mutts would have rushed right to her and tried to overwhelm her with kisses and hugs. Me? I wanted to give my charm a chance to do its magic, slowly and quietly, like the unfolding of a perfect rose in the Garden of Life as the new day's sun spilled rays of fresh yellow light over the horizon of ...

Hmm. I seem to have lost my train of thought. What were we talking about? Bones? No. The weather? I don't think so.

It's funny how that happens. You get all wrapped up in a thought and the next thing you know . . . dingo, it's gone. *Bingo,* not dingo. A dingo is a wild dog, did you know that? It's true. Dingoes live in a place called . . . what's the name of that place? It's south of here, and the whole country is crawling with kangaroos.

Actually, it might be incorrect to say that the country is *crawling* with kangaroos, because kangaroos don't crawl. They hop, and we're talking about serious hopping. They hop for a living. All day, every day, they hop around.

Oh, and they have pouches, too, right in front of their stomach. Creatures with pouches are called Marsh Soup Eels. Why? I have no idea. Ask a biologist, they're the ones who come up with names that are hard to pronounce, such as Marsh Soup Eels.

My best guess is that kangaroos live in marshes, eat a lot of soup, and have a long tail that resembles an eel, but the important thing is that a mother kangaroo carries her baby around in the pouch, see, which means that baby kangaroos don't do much hopping.

Australia. That's the name of the place that has all the kangaroos, and they've got dingoes, too. Remember dingoes? Wild dogs. They eat kangaroos and kangaroos eat soup, so you might say that dingoes have a super diet.

Ha ha.

A little humor there. Did you get it? Soup and super. Ha ha. Okay, maybe it wasn't all that great but ... what were we talking about before you got me on the subject of kangaroos? Why should a dog in Texas be talking about kangaroos anyway? I've never even seen one, so ...

Wait, hold everything! We were discussing Miss Beulah the Collie. Okay, now we're cooking.

The point is that once a guy has feasted his eyes on Miss Beulah, he'll never think about kangaroos again, even if he recently wolfed down a half-pound of frozen meat. He won't care if they eat soup or salad or hamburgers, because ... you know, I caught a whiff of those burgers on the grill, and you talk about a great smell! A cloud of meat smoke drifted over me and ...

You can eat all the frozen hamburger you want, but give me beef cooked on a grill. Have we mentioned that as a wee little pup, I was raised in a beef box? It's true, that was my nursery. A lot of your ordinary mutts spend their first months of life in a box that's used for shipping oranges or spinach, but you'd never catch a cowdog hanging out in a spinach box. Dogs that are raised in spinach boxes and grapefruit boxes turn out to be little yip-yips, whereas your cowdogs develop a more refined ...

I needed to check out those burgers. Sometimes at a picnic the cooks will, you know, give out free samples, if you approach them just right, and I figured I might as well, uh, test the waters, so to speak.

I followed the fragrant clouds of smoke and headed straight for the barbecue grill. Three men wearing aprons and cowboy hats stood over the fire, talking, sweating, and flipping yummy patties of beef. I approached one of them, sat at his feet, and beamed him an expression that said, *"If only I had a burger, my life would be complete."*

He didn't notice. I mean, the guy had twenty burgers on the grill and he was pretty busy, so I inched closer, swept my tail across the ground, and began making Sounds of Yearning.

At last he noticed me and even smiled (good sign). "Hi, pooch. Are you having a good Fourth of July?"

Oh yes, very nice . . . although . . .

"I guess you want a sample, huh?"

A hamburger? Gee, I hadn't thought of that, but . . . well, one little burger might be a great way to celebrate the holiday. Or even two.

He slipped his splattular . . . splattula . . . spatula . . . whatever you call that thing . . . he slipped it under one of the yummy sizzling burgers, and you know, all at once things inside my body began leaping. My ears leaped up, my eyes leaped open, and my tongue leaped out of my mouth, all in the same instant of time.

He gave me a pleasant smile (this guy liked dogs, I could tell) ... he gave me a pleasant smile and said, "Now, this is going to be hot, so you'll need to ..."

Yes?

His pleasant expression collapsed into one that ... yipes ... wasn't so pleasant. In fact, it became downright ugly, and he said, "Dog, you stink! Get out of here before you ruin the meat. Hyah!"

Fine. I didn't want his greasy old burgers anyway. They were probably burned to a crypt and oversalted and overpeppered, and if he didn't want to share his meat with a loyal, hardworking ranch dog, that was fine with me. Hey, I was no beggar.

And besides, I had more important things to do, such as laying some heavy-duty charm on the World's Most Gorgeous Collie Gal. Maybe you'd forgotten about her and maybe I had, too, just for a minute or two when we got sidetracked on that discussion about kangaroos, but you have to admit that they're pretty interesting little brutes. I kind of wish we had a few of them in Texas, but we don't.

The impointant point is that I stuck with my plan to approach the lady in a . . . hmmm, I almost said, "in a stealthy manner," but that would sound cold and clackulating, wouldn't it? Let's say that I approached her "with reserve" and kept my distance. That sounds better, doesn't it? Of course it does.

Yes, instead of blundering over to her, I stopped about ten feet away and waited for her to feel my presence and discover me in her own time. See, you can't rush these things. True love needs time to grow and develop, because . . . well, because women are pretty strange.

I hate to put it that way, but everything in my experience says it's true. For example, if you want to capture the heart and mind of a cat, it's simple. You wade in, beat him up, and chase him up a tree. At that point, you've won his heart and mind. Or, if you haven't, you don't care because you have parked his heart and mind in a tree, and that's the very best place to park the local cat. Hee hee.

I know all about this stuff, because I do it all the time and it's a blast.

But that approach doesn't work on the womenfolk. Try chasing your girlfriend up a tree and see what happens. It will come back to bite you every time. The ladies need time and space. They need to be courted and charmed, and that's exactly what I had in mind for You-Know-Who.

Hencely, I kept my distance and waited for her to see me. She seemed pretty distracted, watching all the action at the picnic, but I was in no hurry. Time was on my side, see, because the Birdly Wonder wasn't in his usual spot, sitting beside her and behaving like the idiot he truly was.

Heh heh. I could wait and let events unfoliate in their own time.

Whilst I waited, I took the opportunity to primp a bit and improve my appearance. Appearance is important to the ladies, don't you see, and you don't want to show up looking like a ragamuffin—hair sticking up, ears crooked, sandburs in your tail, dog food crumbs on your chops. Those are the signs of a ragamuffin, and the ladies aren't impressed by such things.

It was my good fortune that I had positioned myself right beside a pickup with rounded chrome hubcaps. That was a piece of good luck, because those chrome hubcaps work like a mirror. I could see my reflection in the shiny surface, and it's common knowledge that when you want to slick yourself up, you need a mirror. I had me a mirror, a good mirror, and I stood before it and studied . . .

Good grief, was my nose really that big?

I'd always taken a lot of pride in my long cow-dog nose, but what I was seeing in the mirror shook my pride down to the roots. My nose was HUGE, five times its normal size!

Gulp.

My mind raced back to the events of the past several days, as I tried to imagine what had caused this catastrophe. Was it something I ate? Had I come in contact with some dreaded virus that had attacked my face and twisted it into horrible shapes?

How could I present myself to the Woman of My Dreams, when my face—the only face I'd ever owned—had been transformed into something ugly and grotesque?

I was lost in these dark thoughts when I heard footsteps coming up behind me. I hoped with all my heart that it wasn't Beulah. If she saw me in this condition ... hey, good looks aren't everything in this life, unless your nose resembles a big sausage and when that happens, buddy, *looks matter* and you've got big problems.

I turned and saw to who or whom the footsteps belonged. Drover. He was wearing a long face and shaking his head. "Hank, I tried to tell Slim about the robber, but he didn't understand. Maybe you'd better ..."

"Never mind the robber. Something terrible has happened to me."

He wrinkled up his nose and made a sour face. "Yeah, you smell like a skunk."

"Why do you keep bringing that up?"

"Well . . . because you keep smelling like a skunk . . . and it's hard to ignore."

"Never mind the skunk. It's the least of my worries. Something awful has happened to my face. Look at my nose."

He narrowed his eyes and looked closer. "What about it?"

"It's been disfigured. The skunk spray must have contained some kind of poison that causes flesh to grow into ugly shapes."

"What makes you think so?"

"I saw my face in the mirror." I pointed to the hubcap.

Drover moved toward the mirror and stared at his face. "I'll be derned, that's about the ugliest nose I ever saw."

"See? Now you know the awful truth."

"Yeah, but it's *my* nose, not yours. Do you reckon . . ."

"Drover, we've been friends for a long time. I need your help."

"Yeah, but ..."

"I can't allow Miss Beulah to see me in this condition."

"Hank, that's MY NOSE in the mirror."

I gave him a ferocious glare. "Drover, stop thinking of yourself. We'll deal with your nose tomorrow. Today, we must deal with mine. Is that asking too much?"

He shrugged. "Whatever you think."

I paced a few steps away and gazed off into the distance. "You must carry a message to Miss Beulah."

"I thought you said I couldn't talk to her."

"Everything has changed. My life will never be the same again." I paused a moment to gather my thoughts. "Will you give her an important message?"

"Oh sure, be glad to." He started walking away.

"Come back here! I haven't given you the message yet." He came back and sat down. "All right, here's the message: 'Beulah, my spotless dove, I hath noticed that you came to the picnic without Plato. My heart rejoiceth and singeth, but I'm not able to see you at this time. Please hold my place in line. Signed, Your Dearly Beloved Hank.' Can you remember all of that?"

"Oh yeah, it'll be easy."

"Drover, I want the message delivered exactly as I dictated it. This is extremely important, and my very future depends on it."

He was grinning and hopping up and down. "I've got it. You'll be proud. Here I go!"

He scampered away from the pickup, heading straight for Miss Beulah. I had a bad feeling about this, but . . . well, you'll see.

CHAPTER TEN

Terrible Damage to My Nose

Drover scampered over to where Miss Beulah was sitting in the shade of a big elm tree, while I hid behind the left rear tire of the pickup and listened, hoping against hope that the runt would deliver my message just as I had delivered it—from the depths of my heart.

As he drew closer to Miss Beulah, he began thrashing his ridiculous stub of a tail. She pulled her gaze away from the picnic and smiled at him. "Oh, hello, Drover."

On hearing her voice, he blushed and gasped, fell down and started kicking all four legs, just the kind of silly response you'd expect him to have in the presence of a lady. But at last he managed to climb back to his feet.

So far, so good. I lifted both ears and tried to pick up every word.

"Hi, Miss Beulah. I've got an important message from Hank."

"A message from Hank?" She glanced around. "Is he here?"

"Yes ma'am, but he can't see you right now, and he wanted me to give you this message." He plopped his bohunkus down on the grass and launched into his speech: "'Beulah, my spotless buzzard, I hath noticed that you . . .'"

Beulah frowned. "Wait. Are you sure he said 'spotless buzzard'?"

"Well, let me think here. Maybe it was 'spotted buzzard.'"

"'Spotted buzzard'? What is that supposed to mean?"

"Well, I'm not sure. No, wait. I think it was 'spotless dove.'"

She smiled. "Oh, that's better. Please go on."

Drover gazed up at the sky with dreamy eyes. "'I see that thou hast cometh to the picnic without Plato, and I wisheth that thou wouldst be Drover's girlfriend.' That's the message from Hank, Miss Beulah."

WHAT?

I should have known he couldn't be trusted.

The little thief was writing his own script and trying to steal my girl! I cringed at the thought of going out in public with my deformed nose, but if I didn't take control of this situation, my love life would be wrecked.

I could only hope that she would look beyond my handicap and see the Dog Behind the Nose. I took a deep gulp of air and marched out into the light of day. "Drover, that's enough of your lies! You're dismissed. Go to your room immediately."

"Yeah, but . . ."

"Leave! I'll deal with you later, you ungrateful wretch." He ducked his head and tail and slipped away. I turned my gaze to the Lady of My Dreams. "Miss Beulah, I didn't want you to see me in this condition, but it's become necessary."

She sniffed the air and frowned. "Do you smell something?"

"You see, I had a terrible accident this morning, and I fear my nose will never be the same again."

She looked at me for a long moment. "Really?"

"Yes ma'am, I've been disfigured, like the Humpback of Notary Public." She giggled. "Beulah, I'm shocked that you would laugh at a time like this."

"I think you mean the Hunchback of Notre Dame."

"That's the guy. The world saw only his outward appearance, which was ugly, but his heart was pure as gold. I can only hope that you will look past this poor ruined nose of mine and see the goodness deep inside."

Again, she stared at me for a long time. "When did you first notice your 'poor ruined nose'?"

"Moments ago, when I happened to catch a glimpse of my face in the mirror."

"Which mirror?"

"That hubcap over there." I pointed to the chrome hubcap. To my astonishment, she started laughing again. "Beulah, your laughter pierces my heart like a dagger."

She turned away from me, gasped for air, and kept on laughing. "I'm sorry, Hank, but this is hilarious!"

"Madame, it's not hilarious to those of us who have been maimed."

She was laughing so hard, she fell down and pounded the ground with her paw. "Don't you see what happened? That hubcap has a round surface. It distorts the image."

"Huh? You mean ..."

"Your nose hasn't changed. It's the same nose you've always had."

"That's absurd."

"Look again."

I stalked over to the hubcap and peered at the image. Yipes! This time, what I saw wasn't a huge nose but a huge EYE, and we're talking about something you'd see staring at you from a dead fish. In other words ...

Okay, false alarm. Ha ha. See, that chrome hubcap was rounded and it ... I don't know what it did, but the point is that my nose was okay. Whew! Boy, it had me shook up for a minute or two.

I cut my eyes from side to side and tried to calm the stampede inside my head. "Miss Beulah, this is very embarrassing."

Between chirps of laughter, she managed to gasp, "I'm sure it is."

"It's all coming clear now. Drover tricked me, in hopes that he could steal you away, but now we know the truth." I pulled myself up to my full height and beamed her a rakish smile. "Beulah, it appears that you've finally ditched your bird-dog boyfriend and ... well, I'm here to take his place."

She stopped laughing and looked into my eyes. "Oh, Hank, Plato's gone again. He's off on another quest, and nobody's seen him in two days."

"Hey, great news! The last time he did this, I was foolish enough to bring him back alive. This time ..."

Her eyes blazed at me. "Don't say it! I won't stand for you saying hateful things about poor Plato."

"Poor Plato, my foot! He's an idiot and he's caused me nothing but misery, and I'm thrilled beyond words that . . ." I noticed that her eyes had wandered. It appeared that she was looking at something off to the north. "Excuse me, but I'm in the middle of an important speech."

She kept her eyes focused to the north and brought a paw to her lips. "Shhhh. Look!"

"Beulah, I don't want to look at anything but your lovely face, and frankly, I'd rather you didn't tell me to hush."

There was a long moment of silence, then she turned to me with a radiant smile, and I mean a smile that lit up the whole world. And she gasped, "Everything has worked out!"

"Well, thank goodness! I'm glad you've finally . . ."

"It's HIM! He's come back!"

Huh? Who?

I squinted toward the north and saw my life falling into ruins before my very eyes. Would you like to guess who was coming toward us, limping through the picnic ground? It was the same dingbat, stick-tailed spotted bird-dog jerk who had been off on a quest to find the Great White Quail . . . but instead of getting himself bumped off by a pack of hungry coyotes, it was my bad luck that he'd found his way back to civilization.

With a mounting sense of outrage, I watched as Beulah rushed out to meet the buffoon. "Oh, Plato, I've been so worried!"

With his tongue hanging out the left side of his mouth, he gave her the dumbest smile I'd ever seen and yelled, "Honeybun! I'm just in time for the picnic, huh? Great!" He saw me and gave me the same idiot grin. "Hank! Hey, great to see you again! You're looking good, fella." He gave me a wink. "Clean living, huh? Great."

In the privacy of my mind, I said . . . I won't tell you what I said, but I can assure you that it wasn't nice.

The moron limped into the pool of shade and collapsed. Beulah hovered over him, casting worried glances. "Poor dear, you're wounded! What have you done to yourself?"

"It's nothing, Sweetsie."

"Plato, you have cactus spines in your feet."

He scowled at one of his paws, which resembled a pin cushion. "By golly, no wonder they hurt."

"And you're as thin as a snake! When was the last time you ate anything?"

He frowned. "You know, I have no idea, probably days. I forget about food when I'm out on a quest."

She gave him a pat. "I'll see if I can find you some scraps. You and Hank can talk."

"Great. Thanks a gob, Sweetums." She left and he turned to me. "You know, Hank, when I'm off on a quest, my mind seems to shift into a different dimension."

"No kidding."

"I mean, it's as though I'm looking at everything through a tiny lens."

"How interesting."

"Right, and I don't even notice other details, such as . . . well, hunger and thirst and walking through a whole bunch of cactus." He leaned toward me. "Hank, I was on the trail of the most amazing covey of blue quail you ever dreamed of."

"I don't dream of quail."

"There must have been thirty-forty birds, just a magnificent covey!"

"I'll swan."

"But you know about blue quail. They run. They took off running and led me on a merry . . ."

Suddenly I had an idea. I cut him off. "Plato, what happened to your nose?"

He looked at me and after a few seconds, his vapid eyes drifted into focus. "I beg your pardon?"

I glanced over both shoulders and whispered, "Something terrible has happened to your nose. It's grotesque, deformed. I guess Beulah didn't want to mention it."

He put a paw to his nose and felt around. "My nose? Golly, I didn't notice anything."

"Plato, when you're off chasing birds, you lose touch with reality. Remember?"

"That's true, it really is. So . . . my nose? Something's happened to it?"

"Yes, and I'm sorry to be the one to give you the bad news. You might even want to . . . well, leave the picnic."

His jaw dropped. "That bad?"

"That bad. Beulah will never tell you this, but I'm sure she's embarrassed to be seen with you."

He gasped. "Good heavens! I don't want to be a burden."

"I know you don't, Plato. Here, come look at your face in this mirror." I steered him over to the chrome hubcap. "Brace yourself and take a look."

Heh heh. I guess you've figured out my Plan for Plato. Heh heh. The mind of a cowdog is an awesome thing.

My Wicked Plan for Plato's Future

You probably think it was cruel of me to take advantage of the birdbrain, and maybe it was, but I didn't care. The jerk had caused me misery for years, having stolen my woman and broken my heart into sixty-two pieces, and if I had to cheat to win back Miss Beulah, so be it.

He squinted at his face in the mirror . . . and you should have been there! Ho, it was the funniest thing I'd seen in years. His eyes flew open and his jaw went all the way to the floor. When he finally was able to speak, he gasped, "Good grief, you're right. It looks awful!"

I laid a paw upon his trembling shoulder—a true friend in his moment of greatest darkness, heh heh. "There, there. I'm sure it will heal."

"You think so?"

"Oh sure. Give it a couple of years, and it'll be fine."

"A couple of years! Hank, bird season starts in two months! What if I can't hunt?"

"One thing at a time, old buddy. Right now, we need to get you away from here." I began easing him along. "I know you don't want to embarrass Beulah."

"Right. No, Hank, I'd rather be flogged."

"That can be arranged."

"Excuse me?"

"Let's hurry, before she comes back."

"Right." I steered him south, toward the creek. We had gone several steps when he stopped, cocked his head to the side, and blinked his eyes. "Wait a second. I just had an interesting thought."

"Uh, Plato, we'd better . . ."

"Just one second, Hank, I need to check something." He rushed back to the hubcap and looked at himself again. He threw back his head and started laughing. "Hank, great news! I just figured it out. The surface of the hubcap distorts the image!"

"That's impossible."

"No, it's true. What we're seeing isn't real. Here, come look for yourself." I didn't need to "look for myself," but I did, just to keep up appearances. Plato laughed and whopped me on the back. "By golly, Hank, you really had me scared there for a minute . . ."

He froze. His foppish grin melted, and he lifted his famous bird-dog nose. He sniffed the air several times, and slowly his gaze drifted around to . . . well, to me, it seemed.

His face turned serious. "Hank, we're friends, right? I mean, we can talk, man to man, dog to dog?"

"What's your point?"

He glanced over both shoulders and lowered his voice. "Hank, only a friend would tell you this. You . . . you have an *odor problem*."

For a moment of heartbeats, I couldn't decide whether I should laugh in his face or beat him up, so I said, "I got sprayed by a skunk. So what?"

He scowled and pursed his lips. "Hank, I know Beulah pretty well and . . . Hank, let me be candid. She doesn't like the smell of skunk." He lowered his voice to a confidential tone. "A bath might be good, Hank, and I say that in all sincerity."

I pushed him away. "Dunce! If you're such an expert on women, how come you keep running off to chase quail?"

His eyes went blank. "Hank, I don't know how to answer that."

"Good, because I'm tired of hearing you blabber. Here she comes, and we'll see what she says. I'll bet she doesn't even notice the smell."

Beulah came toward us in a trot, carrying a piece of hamburger bun in her mouth. She laid it at Plato's feet and gave him such a sugary smile, it almost made me sick. "There, you poor thing. That will keep you alive until . . ." Her words hung in the air. She lifted her nose and sniffed. Her gaze turned like . . . well, it kind of reminded me of a gun turret of one of those battleships, turning toward a target. She stabbed me with her gaze. "Skunk?"

"Beulah, my dumpling, I think I can explain everything."

Her eyes burst into flames. "You smell HORRIBLE!"

"Yes, well . . ."

"How dare you come to a picnic . . . oh-h-h-h!" She whirled around to Plato. "Tell your friend to take a bath before he goes out in public!"

Plato nodded. "Right. I already told him."

She stuck her nose in the air and stalked away with short angry steps.

Maybe I should have left it there, but . . . well, I

didn't. I raised my voice and yelled, "So that's the kind of woman you are, huh? Appearances and superficial stuff? Fine, Beulah, and you know what? I think it's finished between us!"

Over her shoulder, she snapped, "Get a date with a skunk!"

Plato gave his head a sad shake. "You know, Hank, she's right. You really should ..."

"Will you please shut your trap?"

"Well, sure, Hank, if that's how you feel. I was just ..."

"I have a ranch to run, and you're wasting my time. I hope you enjoy your cactus." I wheeled around and marched away.

Behind me, I heard him call out, "Great seeing you again, Hank. And don't forget, dove season starts September the first! Take care!"

Dove season. What a loser!

But you know what really ripped me? If Plato was such a loser, how come he always ended up with my girlfriend? It was one of the great mysteries of my life and a source of irremuckable sadness.

Oh well, I had important work to do. Had you forgotten that we were in the midst of a major investigation? Not me. Okay, maybe it had slipped my mind for a few minutes, but I was back on the case and ready to take charge.

See, I still had to get the message to Slim that his house had been burgled. I had assigned that job to Drover, but of course he'd made a mess of it. I should have known.

And speaking of Mister Squeakbox, guess who appeared out of nowhere and fell in step beside me. Drover. He gave me his patented silly grin. "Oh, hi. How'd it go with Beulah?" I didn't answer or even look at him. "She told you to get a date with a skunk, so maybe it didn't go too well."

"I'm ignoring you."

"Yeah, I noticed."

"And you *will* be court-martialed."

"Gosh, what did I do?"

"Everything. The list of charges is a mile long, but the trial will last only thirty seconds. You will spend the next fifty years with your nose in the corner."

"I hate standing with my nose in the corner."

"Good. I'll enjoy every second of your misery."

"Are you looking for Slim?"

"No." I stopped and ran my gaze over the crowd at the picnic. "Yes. Where is he?"

"If I tell, will you shorten my sentence?"

"Drover, bribery is a serious crime."

"Yeah, but will it work?"

I gave that a moment's thought. "Okay, twenty-five years. Where is he?"

He pointed his paw toward a group of people sitting in lawn chairs. "He's over there with Miss Viola. I think they're fixing to play a song."

The very mention of Miss Viola caused my spirits to rise. You might remember that she was very fond of me. There were rumors that she and Slim were sweet on each other, but I knew the truth. She adored ME and tolerated Slim because . . . well, because he was my friend, I suppose.

Yes, Viola and I had always been able to communicate our deepest thoughts and feelings. If Slim wasn't able to understand my message about the burglar, I was pretty sure that I could get it across to Viola. And, hey, she might even give me a bite of her homemade ice cream. Heh heh.

I turned back to Drover. "Get your affairs in order, you'll be spending the next twenty-five years in prison."

"Could we shorten it to ten minutes?"

I wrestled with this heavy moral delemon. "Will you promise never to lock me out of the house again?"

"Well, I didn't actually lock you out. You just couldn't open the door."

I stuck my nose in his face. "All right, then promise to stop learning tricks that I can't do. Promise or rot in jail!"

"Okay, I promise."

"Good. We'll skip the court-martial. Go to your room and stick your nose in the corner."

"Five minutes?"

"That's correct, and don't try to cheat. I'll be watching."

He trotted down to the gas tanks to begin serving his time. I hated to be so stern with the little mutt, but there were lessons he needed to learn.

I turned myself toward the north and marched straight over to the shady spot where Slim and Viola were sitting in a circle with several other people. Slim had brought out his banjo and was tuning it up. Viola picked up her mandolin and started playing a little bluegrass number called "Wild Plum Jelly." I sat down and listened.

My goodness, she was pretty good on that thing, and Slim didn't sound too bad on the banjo either. They made nice music together.

When it was over, she smiled and nodded to the crowd of people who broke into applause. I found myself thinking, "Hey, a lady with that kind of talent needs a loyal dog who will lie at her feet and gaze up at her with adorning eyes and guard her mandolin."

That's exactly what she needed, and I just happened to have a particular dog in mind for the job. ME.

With that thought blazing in my mind, I pretty muchly forgot that I was in the middle of an important investigation and was supposed to be warning Slim about the crook who'd broken into his house.

Sliding through the crowd, I went straight to Miss Viola, laid my head upon her lap, and gave her a look that said, "Hi. I hear you've been looking all over for me."

CHAPTER TWELVE

A Very Dramatic Ending, Wow!

She saw me. Her eyes softened and began to shine with the light of love. When she smiled, all the burdens and tragedies in my life fell away like . . . something. When she reached out her tender hand and laid it upon my head, I felt as though I'd been struck by a paralyzing ray.

After a moment, I was able to flash her a message in Tailwag: "Viola, dearest lady, don't waste your time with Slim. He's nothing but a bachelor who sits on the porch in his shorts and sings corny songs. I, on the other hand, am the dog you've been waiting for all your life."

I held my breath and waited for her reply. She let out a groan and shrieked, "Hank, you smell terrible! Skunk, yuck!"

I heard Slim's voice behind me. "Hank, for crying out loud!"

I didn't care. He could yell all he wanted. I knew that Viola would understand and that's all that ... her eyes grew wide and her face turned to ice.

I was stunned. She pushed me away. For the first time in our relationship, *she pushed me away*! And it got even worse. She clapped a hand over her nose and said, "Hank, I'm sorry, but I can't take that smell!"

Yes, but what about loyalty and devotion? Didn't those qualities matter any more?

Slim leaped out of his chair and towered over

me like a thundercloud. "Hank, how many times do you have to get skunked before you learn?"

Skunked? Oh yes, the skunk, which reminded me that I had a very important message to deliver. I turned to Slim and began transmitting in Tailwag. "Slim, some guy with a trained skunk walked into your ..."

"Go on, get out of here! Scat!"

He wasn't listening! Nobody understood the truth, that I had been skunked while protecting the ranch. With my head and tail dragging the ground, I turned and walked away. My heart had been skewered.

Pretty sad, huh? You bet. It was one of the darkest moments of my whole career. I had been dumped by two girlfriends and rejected by the man I had thought was my dearest friend in the world—all in the same afternoon.

Groan. Oh well, the damage was done. I'd had my chance to deliver the message and I'd blown it. The investigation was finished. I was finished. Until I got rid of the skunk smell, I would have no job and no friends.

I had gone about ten steps toward a hopeless future when I heard Slim's voice behind me. "Wait a second! Skunk? Hank, come back here!" I stopped and looked back at him. He came toward me with long strides. "Hank, did somebody show up at my house after I left?"

I delivered one loud bark. Yes!

"And did he have a pet skunk?"

Another loud bark. Yes!

He turned to Viola. "Good honk, it's that crook Bobby Kile told me about. He's in the neighborhood."

I delivered another loud bark that said, "It sure took you long enough to figure it out! I came within an inch of resigning from the Security Division, and then you'd have had a real mess on your hands."

I'm not sure Slim got that message. In fact, I'm pretty sure that he didn't, because he took off in a long trot to find Loper and told him about the robber. The two of them went to the house and placed a phone call to the sheriff's office.

Twenty minutes later, Chief Deputy Kile pulled into Ranch Headquarters in his Holstein-colored sheriff's car (black and white, like a Holstein cow). After a short conference among the three of them, the deputy climbed back into his car. Loper brought up one of the ranch's pickups, and Slim called me up for active duty.

"Come on, pooch. You might as well ride along . . . just in case."

Just in case? I wasn't sure what he meant by that, but who cared? Hey, the important thing was that I was back in the saddle and back on the case. I rushed to the pickup door and waited for Slim to . . .

"Uh-uh. You ride in the back, Stink Bomb. You might end this day as a hero, but right now you're in Skunk Quarantine."

Fine, no problem there. I didn't mind riding in the back. I leaped up into the bed of the pickup, took my place of honor in the middle of the spare tire, and off we went to Slim's place, two miles down the creek.

And my name wasn't "Stink Bomb."

When we got there, it didn't take them long to pick up the clues. The area in front of the saddle shed still reeked of skunk perfume and there was . . . oops, the empty wrapper of what had once been a package of hamburger meat.

Slim picked up the wrapper between a finger and thumb and shot me a dark scowl. I beamed him an innocent smile that said, "Well, what did you expect?" He grinned. I think he understood. If he'd been a dog, he would have eaten it, too.

By then, Deputy Kile had found some boot prints in the dust and we followed the trail north, into a grove of chinaberry trees. On the other side of the grove, he stopped and shook his head. "Ground's too hard. I've lost him."

The ground was too hard? Ha. Who needed footprints? I pushed my way to the front, put my nose to the ground, and began following the trail that led off to the northwest. See, I didn't have the best nose in the world, but tracking a skunk wasn't a problem. Even Drover could have followed that trail.

I led them through a stand of hackberry trees and up into a rocky ravine. The scent was growing stronger and suddenly I looked up and saw ... my goodness, it appeared to be a little hut made of limbs and branches. I stopped and pointed like a flaming arrow.

Behind me, the deputy said, "There we go! Nice work, pup." He cupped a hand around his mouth and shouted, "Okay, buddy, you've got company! Sheriff's department. Come out with your hands in the air!"

Inside the hut, we heard a voice. "Shove off! You can come in if you want, but you'll get skunked! I've got a gas mask. How about you?"

The deputy scowled and hitched up his belt. "Anybody want to volunteer to go in?" Dead silence. Slim and Loper looked up at the sky. The deputy pulled on his chin and kicked a rock with his boot. He was quiet for a long time, then his head came up and there seemed to be a twinkle in his eyes. "Slim, what's the dog's name?"

"Bozo."

"What's his name?"

"Hank."

The deputy knelt down and slapped a hand on his thigh. "Come here, Hank. Say, you look like a fine dog."

Hey, did you hear that? A fine dog! I hoped that Slim and Loper were listening.

I went to the officer, and he rubbed me behind the ears. "Hank, how would you like to go to work for me?"

I was amazed, speechless. Go to work for the sheriff's department? Become a genuine police dog? Hey, that would be SO COOL! Yes, yes, and yes!

He held my head in his hands and looked into my eyes. "Okay, bud, I've got a job for you, a very important job. I can't trust Loper or Slim to carry it out."

Oh, I understood that. They were a couple of goof-offs. Give 'em an assignment, and all they want to do is make jokes and pull pranks. He didn't need to tell me about Slim and Loper. I knew them very well.

He rose to his feet, wrinkled up his nose, and fanned the air in front of his face. "Hank, I've never hired anyone that smelled quite as bad as you, but I think you're the right man for this job. Are you ready?"

I drew myself up to my full height of massiveness. "Aye, aye, sir. Lock and load!"

Huh? That was odd. He wrapped his arms around my middle and picked me up and started walking toward the...what were we doing? Surely he wasn't planning to ... *hey, there was a loaded skunk inside that hut*!

I guess you've figured it out by now. Deputy Kile pitched me inside, and in that instant before my feet hit the floor, I caught a glimpse of the enemy. It was like a photograph, a moment frozen in time. Leland was sitting along the north wall, adjusting the elastic straps on his gas mask and getting ready to put it over his face. His skunk sat nearby, nibbling on some potato peelings. The expression on the crook's face told me that he had been caught by surprise.

And then things began happening pretty fast. Rosebud saw me, fanned out his tail, whipped around in my direction, hiked himself up on his front legs, and took dead aim at me.

I heard Leland croak, "Rosebud, not yet!"

Rosebud wasn't listening and started shooting. It was another of those rolling balls of something yellow and awful. BLAP! I got plastered, and so did everything inside that hut, including the owner of the skunk. By the time he got the gas mask pulled over his face, it was too late.

I don't remember any of the details, only that I gagged and staggered out of the hut and started looking for fresh air. The crook was only a step behind me and he walked right into a pair of handcuffs. Wow, what a finish! I had broken the case and caught the bad guy—who, by the way, stunk so bad they had to haul him to jail in the back of Loper's pickup.

And that's about all the story. I was invited NOT to make another appearance at the picnic and without me there, well, things just fell apart. Beulah cried. Miss Viola cried. Every woman at the picnic cried. For a while, people stood around talking about my daring capture of the outlaw, then they packed up their things and went home.

No fireworks, no more singing or pitching horseshoes. I mean, what's the point of throwing a party if the guest of honor can't attend?

But the important thing is that I had solved the case, saved the ranch, brought the crook to justice, and won a whole shoe box full of medals and ribbons. And fellers, that's as good as it gets around here. This case is ...

Wait, hold everything. You're probably wondering what happened to Rosebud, the Secret Weapon. Okay, here's the scoop on that. In all the confusion, he walked away, scot-free, but two weeks later, I caught the little creep trying to steal some of our dog food and ... never mind.

Too many encounters with a skunk can mess up a happy ending, so let's just say that I had learned my lesson about skunks and never saw him again.

And with that, this case is closed.

The following activities are samples from *The Hank Times,* the official newspaper of Hank's Security Force. Do not write on these pages unless this is your book. Even then, why not just find a scrap of paper?

"Photogenic" Memory Quiz

We all know that Hank has a "photogenic" memory—being aware of your surroundings is an important quality for a Head of Ranch Security. Now you can test your powers of observation.

How good is your memory? Look at the illustration on page 14 and try to remember as many things about it as possible. Then turn back to this page and see how many questions you can answer.

1. Did Slim's boxers have polka dots, hearts, or stripes?

2. What was on the calendar? Horses, mountains, or sailboats?

3. Was the burned match in Slim's right hand or his left hand?

4. How many mice were in the picture? One mouse, two mice, or three meece?

5. What was in the trash can? A can, a bottle, or a rolled up newspaper?

6. How many of Slim's eyes could you see? 1, 2, or 3?

Eye-Crosserosis

I've done it again. I was staring at the end of my nose and had my eyes crossed for a long time. And you know what? They got hung up—my eyes, I mean. I couldn't get them uncrossed. It's a serious condition called Eye-Crosserosis. (You can read about the big problems Eye-Crosserosis caused me in my second book.) This condition throws everything out of focus, as you can see. Can you help me insert the double letters into the word groupings to create words you can find in my books?

DD	**NN**	**BB**	**UU**	**PP**	**DD**
EE	**LL**	**TT**	**FF**	**OO**	**GG**

1. SIY _____

2. PEY _____

3. ES _____

4. CHSE _____

5. MILE _____

6. KIING *__KIDDING__*

7. DISAEAR _____

8. GD-BYE _____

9. BUERFLY _____

10. RUISH _____

11. VACM _____

12. STUING _____

Answers:

1. SILLY
2. PENNY
3. EGGS
4. CHEESE
5. MIDDLE
6. KIDDING
7. DISAPPEAR
8. GOOD-BYE
9. BUTTERFLY
10. RUBBISH
11. VACUUM
12. STUFFING

Have you read all of Hank's adventures?

Join Hank the Cowdog's Security Force

Are you a big Hank the Cowdog fan? Then you'll want to join Hank's Security Force. Here is some of the neat stuff you will receive:

Welcome Package
- A Hank paperback of your choice
- A free Hank bookmark

Eight issues of *The Hank Times* with
- Stories about Hank and his friends
- Lots of great games and puzzles
- Special previews of future books
- Fun contests

More Security Force Benefits
- Special discounts on Hank books and audiotapes
- An original Hank poster (19" x 25") absolutely free
- Unlimited access to Hank's Security Force website at www.hankthecowdog.com

Total value of the Welcome Package and *The Hank Times* is $23.95. However, your two-year membership is **only $8.95** plus $4.00 for shipping and handling.

☐ Yes, I want to join Hank's Security Force. Enclosed is $12.95 ($8.95 + $4.00 for shipping and handling) for my **two-year membership**. [Make check payable to Maverick Books.]

Which book would you like to receive in your Welcome Package? Choose any book in the series.

(#   )   (#   )
_____
FIRST CHOICE   SECOND CHOICE

                                              BOY or GIRL
_____
YOUR NAME   (CIRCLE ONE)

_____
MAILING ADDRESS

_____
CITY   STATE   ZIP

_____
TELEPHONE   BIRTH DATE

_____
E-MAIL

Are you a ☐ Teacher or ☐ Librarian?

Send check or money order for $12.95 to:

Hank's Security Force
Maverick Books
P.O. Box 549
Perryton, Texas 79070

DO NOT SEND CASH. NO CREDIT CARDS ACCEPTED.
Allow 4–6 weeks for delivery.

The Hank the Cowdog Security Force, the Welcome Package, and The Hank Times *are the sole responsibility of Maverick Books. They are not organized, sponsored, or endorsed by Penguin Group (USA) Inc., Puffin Books, Viking Children's Books, or their subsidiaries or affiliates.*